OCACHI'S RUN

The morning Rufus Lobo and his rabble-rousing sidekicks saw the last of the town of Bitters through a haze of smoke and flame was the day four men rode into hell — hell in the shape of a cunning half-breed, one-time Indian scout, Ocachi, who sought revenge for the death of his wife at Lobo's hands. But Ocachi was not the only hell stalking Lobo — following him on a long-standing trail of hatred was Marshal Jim Randall . . .

LUTHER CHANCE

OCACHI'S RUN

Complete and Unabridged

LINFORD
Leicester

First published in Great Britain in 1998 by
Robert Hale Limited
London

First Linford Edition
published 2001
by arrangement with
Robert Hale Limited
London

British Library CIP Data

Chance, Luther
    Ocachi's run.—Large print ed.—
Linford western library
1. Western stories
2. Large type books
I. Title
823.9'14 [F]

ISBN 0–7089–9732–5

Published by
F. A. Thorpe (Publishing)
Anstey, Leicestershire

Set by Words & Graphics Ltd.
Anstey, Leicestershire
Printed and bound in Great Britain by
T. J. International Ltd., Padstow, Cornwall

This book is printed on acid-free paper

This for T. P.
who's always known the
worth of a shadow

1

They thundered through the haze of breaking light and swirling dirt as if hounded by the Devil. Four riders, already sweat-soaked, their faces taut and grizzled behind grey masks of dust, the knuckles of their hands white with the grip on reins to lathered mounts that snorted fire. Only their eyes told of the hell they had left and mirrored the one still to come.

Riding a length ahead of his companions was Rufus Lobo, a middle-aged gunslinger out of Utah whose claim to fame and notoriety through a half-dozen territories lay in his vicious contempt for life at the end of a barrel. Lobo had killed his first man, a deputy sheriff back in Pensville, while still a teenager, and spent the next twenty years not bothering to count the bodies in his ruthless pursuit of money, women and easy living. Nobody crossed Lobo and walked on.

Close on the heels of the leading mount was Mitch Siers, youngest of the group, who had come into the protective grip of Lobo after running from a Bible-preaching father and a drunken mother on a bankrupt homestead in the outback of Nevada. Siers had adapted without so much as blinking to a lifestyle whose only discipline was the word of the man who had given him the freedom to be full grown and taught him the language of gun talk.

Pounding the dirt just back of Siers was Clips Monaghan, a one-time rough rider through Oregon who rated himself the fastest gun and blade this side of Pueblo. Monaghan's first love was rabble-rousing to prove his claim and taking on anyone fool enough to challenge him. His second was reading out aloud the markers of the interns on Boot Hill.

Bringing up the rear of the hard-riding party on this morning was

Gentle Joe Jensen, long-standing side-kick to Lobo and regarded by many as the 'brains' of the group. It was Jensen who did the thinking, who made the plans, plotted the four men's fortunes and, some reckoned, had more than once stood between Lobo and a gun that might have proved too fast. He had earned the nickname 'Gentle' on account of his slow-talking drawl and habit of never seeming to shift out of a one-pace swagger. But that was about the extent of Jensen's gentleness. The rest of him was all rattler.

Four riders breaking through the dawn light of a day that would come up sun-baked and dirt dry. Four men riding from a hell of their own making, each with his own thoughts of how it had come to be in a two-bit drag of a town that had hardly seemed worth the bother . . .

Lobo had been the one to insist they rest easy for the night at Bitters. Place looked half dead, rundown, a back-of-beyond town where four men 'Wanted' in most territories they crossed might eat, drink and sleep peaceful without the need to keep one eye open. Mitch Siers had offered no opinion. He had been just too dog tired to care. Monaghan had muttered something about looking for some action, but reckoned that his empty belly and parched throat rated the priority.

It had fallen to Jensen to ponder the safer tactic of staying on the move, sleeping rough for another couple of nights, leastways until they had dusted that sonofabitch Marshal Randall clean off their tails. 'That fella's gettin' to me,' he had drawled, scanning the lifeless town through the evening dusk from the head of the draw, 'just like some home-lovin' flea. Whole seven days he's been trailin' us, all the way from west of the Passmore, ever since we hit that homestead. T'ain't natural, not even in a lawman like Randall it ain't. I crossed him once before, years back, but what the hell's he plannin' on? Stayin' with us 'til we get sick enough of his shadow to call a showdown? I ain't for tanglin' with him, not yet I ain't, not 'til we're good and ready or he gives up, so I'm for goin' on, spreadin' the dirt 'tween him and us. I say we ride clear of that heap down there and keep goin'.'

Monaghan had tapped the butt of his Colt and grinned. 'Show him to me. Show me this flea-clingin' marshal. I'll settle him for yuh, sure I will, right here if yuh've a hankerin'.'

Lobo had sighed and spat noisily over a rock face. 'F'Crissake, what's with you fellas? One nosy marshal with nothin' better to do than high-tail our backsides — so? So what? Yuh want for me to say we turn right around and go ask Randall to go home, leave us be? Or yuh want for us to go kill him, waste another couple days? Hell, we had marshals on our tails before now, all manner of the scumbags. Randall ain't no different from the others.'

'I ain't so sure,' Jensen had murmured.

'Well, I am,' Lobo had snapped. 'Real sure, and I ain't puttin' m'self about one bit on his account. We go rest easy down there, take whatever the hole's got worth the takin', then we ride on come sun-up. And Randall can wait, go to hell for all I give a damn. Trust me, Joe. Just trust me, eh?'

'Sure,' Jensen had sighed. 'Like yuh say, Rufus — trust yuh.'

But Gentle Joe Jensen had about as much faith in that kind of trust as he had in sleeping easy on a bed of cactus.

★ ★ ★

The few folk still fated to their dirt-scratching life in Bitters had produced food, drink and the promise of blankets on real beds to the men who had ridden in that night. Nobody had protested that the four had no intention of paying, or that they were there to take what they wanted when they wanted it, or, come to that, raised a word much less a hand in reaction to their wilder demands. The scumbags were there, in control, doing what they would do until the time came for them to ride on and give no more thought to the place than they would the dust they trampled. Bitters had seen it all before, felt it, paid the price and slid back to its numbed silence and loneliness as before.

Or it might have been that way had not Clips Monaghan eaten too well, drunk too much and looked to put an edge on his satisfaction with 'some action round here'.

Target of his attention had been the only man in Bitters with courage enough to wear a gun belt and holstered Colt — Will Barton, the ageing, arthritic sheriff who had never had the good sense to throw in his badge while he had the chance. Monaghan had taunted and teased Barton for a whole hour until it was as plain as the sweat glistening proud on the old man's brow that he was riled enough to draw on a fellow half his age whose gun would clear leather faster than a frenzied fly to an open window.

And so he had — leastways made to reach for his gun, maybe seen the soft grin at Monaghan's lips, caught a glimpse of the others grouped round the bottle-laden table in the dismal saloon bar and wondered why not one of them had moved or said a word to quieten their wild-eyed companion. Maybe this was all part of a pattern, something they had seen before, many times, wherever they happened to hole-up.

Will Barton was never going to know. Monaghan's first shot blazed deep into the old man's chest, throwing him across the room, scattering tables and chairs. His second found a spot between the sheriff's eyes in the instant he had half-raised his head. And then only cold silence until Lobo had belched, Siers giggled, Jensen yawned and Monaghan ranged his Colt over the grey-faced, staring onlookers. 'And who's for bein' next?' he had croaked, licking at the sweat on his upper lip.

There had been no more than seconds of the silence deepening, Monaghan sweating, glaring, twitching, before the sudden, searing rush of flame at the far end of the bar took a hold in a soaring blaze of fire. There were moans, gasps, a high scream from a woman hidden in the shadows. Lobo sprang to his feet; Siers rocked back in his chair and crashed to the floor; Jensen stared at the blaze in disbelief, and Monaghan was rolled aside in the rush of folk for the batwings.

But it was in that moment of panic that Monaghan had emptied the Colt in a crazed bout of wild shooting that had downed two men and buried hot lead in the screaming woman's throat.

'Hell, Clips, ain't yuh had enough for one night?' Lobo had roared above the shouts and clatter, and then pushed Siers and Jensen towards the 'wings. Monaghan had stumbled after them, the empty gun still tight in his grip, the fingers of his other hand already scrambling for the knife that would carve his way clear of the inferno.

The four men had watched the fire rage through the huddled two-bit town until it was no more than a smouldering heap of matchwood with hardly a shape standing that might be called a building.

'God knows how that got started,' Lobo had murmured.

'And mebbe He does,' Jensen had answered.

'Weren't worth a cuss, anyhow,' had been Monaghan's epitaph.

And their last sight of Bitters and its haunted folk had been lost in palls of black smoke.

But smoke was never to be far away for the four on their dirt-swirling dash west from the burned-out town. It was there again on that morning, dead ahead of them now as they cleared the plains land and turned for the sprawl of hills and pine forest; a soft, slow curl of grey drifting gently to the brightening light. Dirt-buster's cabin, Lobo had thought, some place to rest up awhile, shake the ash and stench of that town out of their clothes, take in some fresh coffee, then get to figuring where to go next before Monaghan went beserk again. Darn fool; time was fast coming when something would have to be done about him. Something permanent.

But for now that cabin smoke looked real peaceful.

2

Soon after noon on that same day, Bud Ziggers was beating the hell out of his flea-ridden mattress back of the trading post at the foot of the Moccasin mountains.

The beating had become a monthly ritual, ever since the main trail east to west had been deserted by the wagon folk in favour of the railroad and Bud had given up all hope of acquiring himself a new mattress. And so it had come to this: the 'treatment', as Bud referred to it, out here in the baking heat, that would hopefully set the fleas scurrying and give him another three weeks' reasonable sleep. Not that the old mattress would take many more beatings. Nossir, he reckoned, wiping the sweat from his face, she was about all through, worn thin and splitting up. Be lucky if she made it to the fall.

But not all Bud's attention on this day had been on the mattress. Three times he had stepped back, raised a hand to his eyes to shield against the glare, and stared long and hard over the flat land of sand and stone to the fringe of the pine forest way over to the west. Something odd going on out there, he mused, something out of place, different, breaking the pattern.

Sure, he had seen the familiar curl of smoke from Ocachi's cabin come sun-up; first thing he saw every day; always right on time. Half-breed, one-time Indian scout and his Comanche wife were regular kind of folk, lived their lives according to their rules, and nothing varied. Why should it? They had a clean, decent home out there in the cabin. Cool through the summer, warm come the snows. Ocachi had built it with his own hands, soon after he had finished with the army and settled down with that nice little gal of his. Real home-loving couple they had turned out too. No young ones as yet, but there would be, you could bet on it.

Meantime, pair of them visited the post every couple of months or so, collected whatever Bud had to offer — and paid for it — and went back to their peaceful living, part white style but still Comanche at its roots. Fine folk. Not that Bud had ever got to hearing how Ocachi came to be a breed, and not that it mattered, all he did know was that he had been the finest, shrewdest, most respected scout this side of the Moccasins and done a hell of a lot to help both Indians and settlers. His kind did not come often — and you could mark it if you ever crossed him. Yessir! Fellow had never forgotten his Comanche upbringing, not by a half . . .

But there was something wrong this morning.

How come there was still smoke from the cabin this time of day, and how come it seemed to be getting thicker as if Ocachi was setting flame to half the forest? Not like him; out of character.

And another thing, how come Bud was as near certain as damn it he had seen horses running free far end of the screes? Looked awfully like Ocachi's bunch from here.

Still, maybe there was nothing to it and he had been mistaken.

Back to the mattress and them two aged trappers he had resting up indoors. Hell, they sure knew how to sink their whiskey, second-rate as it was. Came of spending all that time in the mountains. No place for a fellow, unless he could read them like Ocachi could. Oh, yes, Ocachi knew his mountains, sure enough, and them pines. Knew them like he was born to them.

'Darn yuh scratchin' hides!' croaked Bud as he set about beating the mattress again, but still fretting over that thickening smoke.

★   ★   ★

The trappers at Bud Ziggers' trading post were liquored up and snoring in deep sleep by mid afternoon. Bud had long since beaten the fleas from his mattress, and that day might well have slipped to dusk and passed away like any other had it not been for the dust-cloud that thickened out of the pines and turned to the trail heading due east.

Riders — three, could be four — thought Bud, easing his corn-cob pipe between his cracked teeth, and in some hurry. Now just who in hell could they be, and why the rush? He grunted, turned from the window and stepped out to the shaded veranda. Riding hard, a darn sight harder than was necessary in an empty, nowhere land. No place to go, anyhow, before nightfall — save the post, of course. He grunted again, clamped the pipe tight between his teeth and narrowed his eyes on the swirling cloud.

Trouble. He could smell it, just like he had smelled it all day, ever since he had seen the smoke at Ocachi's cabin . . . And there was another thing: there

16

was no smoke now, so why was Ocachi missing out on supper?

Bud Ziggers rolled his shoulders against the sudden cling of sweat across them. Whoever it was out there riding like a ghost wind had come from the direction of the cabin. Ocachi had had visitors. Who? Old army partners? Comanches? Drifters, trappers? Sure decided to leave in a hurry. And why this time of day? Might just as well have settled for the night. Nearest bed from here on was more than twenty miles away. Unless these fellows planned on —

Bud swept the pipe from his mouth and blew a line of smoke to the sun-dimming haze. If the riders figured on holing up at the post, they could think again. Bad enough having them trappers cluttering up the place. More bodies would only set them fleas hopping again. Nossir, they would have to ride on, just keep going, go find some other place. And in case they had other ideas, he would go get that old

17

Winchester of his, make it plain as the nose on his face just where he stood. There were times when a fellow had to stake his ground . . .

Bud Ziggers was standing his ground, the rifle cradled casually across his arms, when the riders were finally shapes in the cloud of dust. Mean-eyed foursome, he thought, squinting and sweating as they reined to a slithering halt just short of the post, real rough riders, dirt-streaked and smelling fit to smother the air. They looked like trouble sat square at their backs and had been there for years.

'Easy there,' called the thicker-set rider steadying his mount clear of the others. 'No problem here, mister. Just passin' through.'

Too right you are, thought Bud, and fast!

'Yuh open for business?' called the man again.

'Sure he is,' muttered one of his partners.

'Post's been closed these past two

years,' croaked Bud. 'Ain't no business hereabouts. No folk neither. Place ain't worth a spit.'

'Yuh got company, though,' drawled the man, relaxing in his saddle. 'Seen it for m'self in them mounts and pack mules hitched out back.'

Darn those trappers, cursed Bud inwardly. Should have had them hide their horses. 'Coupla trappers,' he murmured. 'Just waterin' up. Movin' out right now.'

But Bud was already regretting his lame explanation at the sound of the shuffling steps behind him, the heaving cough, rumble of an empty stomach and waft of whiskey-laden breath.

'Wa's goin' on here?' slurred the trapper. 'Wa's all the noise? Fella needs his sleep this time of day . . . '

The riders sat easy, watching the trapper sway to the far end of the veranda, reach wildly for the wall as he lost his balance, and thud against it, blinking drunkenly.

Bud swallowed, sweated, tightened

his grip on the rifle and stared anxiously at the leading rider.

'Well, now,' grinned Lobo, 'look yuh here, fella's all loused up, ain't he? Now I wonder how he got himself like that, eh? He been trappin' tonsil varnish up in them hills or somethin'? I reckon not, eh boys? No way. No, I figure he's been swiggin' right here. That so, Mister Trade Post Man?'

Bud swallowed. 'Well, mebbe I did happen to have — '

'Sure, yuh did, and I reckon there's a whole lot more stashed inside, eh, more than enough for me and my boys?'

'Could be I might rustle up — '

'Yeah, yeah,' smiled Lobo. 'But let's not get greedy. I mean, that fella there's had his fair share, ain't he, and same goes for his partner too, I'd reckon. And seein' as how they're so keen on sleepin' . . . Well, I figure we can accommodate that, can't we?' Lobo's smile faded. 'Clips,' he ordered brusquely, 'see to it, will yuh?'

'My pleasure,' said Monaghan, drawing his Colt.

'Now, yuh hold it right there, mister,' stammered Bud, 'I don't want no — '

The Colt's blaze drew a last, gasping breath from the slumped trapper and brought his partner staggering to the doorway. 'What the hell . . . ?' But Monaghan's second shot had settled like a searing poker in the man's head before his eyes were fully open.

'Easier than killin' that squaw woman back there,' grinned Monaghan, holstering his gun. 'But nothin' like so pleasurable.'

And then Bud Ziggers' blood ran colder than the mountain snows.

3

Bud Ziggers' shivering was shaking his bones to his ankles. Another hour of this, he thought, reaching for a bottle of the cheap, gut-rot whiskey, and he would be a wreck — and worse, he might be too stiff-limbed dead to know it!

He slid the bottle to the cluttered table and stepped back to the shadows. How much more of that poison could them scumbags gulp? They were into their fifth bottle now, and no sign of calling it a night. But maybe he should be grateful for that; minute they stopped drinking they might get to figuring on other diversions. And the selection this night, here in the trading post, was a mite limited.

He shivered again and stared at the four men gathered in the glow of the lantern's smoky light. Which one, he wondered, had done the killing, or had they all taken a hand in the death of Ocachi's wife? Hell, how come she had been alone at the cabin, anyhow? But that hardly mattered now; fact was the woman was dead, the cabin burned to embers, wild horses scattered, and these sonsofbitches were laughing over it, boasting, reliving it as if it had been some game, as callous as hunting down a wounded animal. Had they any notion of what they had done? Damn it, not so much as a snitch! Well, they would — oh, yes, they surely would once Ocachi . . .

Bud gulped as Lobo's eyes settled on him like a hawk's hungry gaze. 'Yuh ain't sayin' a deal, fella,' he growled. 'We upset yuh, or somethin', that yuh trouble? Sorry about yuh trapper friends, but they looked all through, anyhow. So what's eatin' yuh?' His eyes narrowed. 'Yuh know that squaw woman back there? She come visitin', or mebbe yuh visited her, eh? She trade comforts for a bag of beans?' He grinned. 'Yeah, I'll bet! Well, it's goin' to be a cold winter for yuh, fella, and that's for sure!'

Bud gulped again, blinked through the sweat clouding his eyes and stiffened against another shiver. 'Oca-chi's wife,' he murmured, his hands beginning to shake. 'That's who yuh killed. Ocachi's wife . . . '

'And just who the hell is Ocachi?' drawled Monaghan, heaving his feet to the table and leaning back in his chair.

'I ain't never heard of him,' slurred Siers. 'Yuh heard of him, Rufus?'

Lobo wiped a hand across his mouth. 'Never,' he croaked. 'What's he — some worn-out Indian? Sounds it. Say one thing for him, though, he sure knew how to pick himself a squaw! Yuh reckon so, Joe? Ain't had m'self a squaw like her before. Nossir!'

Jensen sat forward to rest his arms on the table and narrowed his gaze on Bud. 'Tell me about this Ocachi, mister,' he said softly. 'Tell me.'

'Ar, what the hell!' groaned Lobo.

24

'Don't matter who he is. I ain't interested.'

'I am,' snapped Jensen. 'I wanna know.'

Bud blinked another surge of sweat clear of his eyes and licked his lips.

'Well, get to it, mister,' said Monaghan. 'We ain't got all night.'

'One-time Indian scout,' began Bud. 'Half-breed. Part Comanche. Worked out of Fort Warsash with Colonel Oliver, then settled back there in the hills when the troubles were over. His . . . his wife, the woman yuh killed, was Red Eye's daughter. That's who she was. Red Eye's first born.'

There was a full half-minute of silence before Lobo shifted again. ' 'Breed's woman,' he muttered. 'Might've known. She had that smell about her. Yuh smell her, Joe?'

Jensen stayed silent, watching Bud's face. 'And where was this Ocachi today, then, mister?' he asked.

'No tellin',' stammered Bud. 'Huntin' mebbe — but that's no matter. It's what yuh left him to find that's goin' to raise the fire of hell. I'm tellin' yuh, mister — '

'Will somebody shut this fella's mouth?' roared Lobo. 'Shut it fast — and now, f'Crissake!'

'Sure,' said Monaghan, sliding his feet from the table.

'Hold it,' ordered Jensen, as Bud backed deeper into the shadows. 'There'll be no more killin' this day. We got other things to reckon on.'

'Not from where I'm sittin' we ain't,' coughed Lobo, reaching for the whiskey bottle. ''Breed's woman don't make no mark in my book, no matter whose daughter she is, and I ain't fussed a mite about this Ocachi fella.'

He gulped the drink and licked his lips. 'Few more hours and we'll be clear of this place, anyhow. Plan headin' north-west. There's a town outa here name of — '

'What about Randall?' asked Jensen with a quick, sharp shift of his gaze to Lobo's eyes. 'Yuh reckoned on him?'

Lobo thudded the bottle back to the table. 'There yuh go again, frettin' yuh butt over that scavengin' marshal we ain't set eyes on in days! What's eatin' yuh with him, f'Crissake?'

'We should wait for the sonofabitch to get here. Take him out then,' drawled Monaghan.

'I'm for that,' agreed Siers.

'I ain't,' snapped Lobo. 'I ain't ratin' him. Never have. Wasted effort. We've had our good time back there at Bitters, and yuh all of yuh shared that squaw woman. Now we get to business. The bank at North Forks — that's where we're headin', and no half-breed grievin' over his woman, or two-bit marshal with itchy sand in his boots is changin' that. North Forks come sun-up. Yuh got it?'

Bud Ziggers swallowed on a dry, pinched throat as his gaze moved over the faces of the four men. What now, he wondered; would they settle for Lobo's planning, or would the hell-fire that was sitting with them flare again? All it needed was one word out of place, a sudden movement, and Lobo would as soon draw his gun as spit across the floor. And that fellow Monaghan was beginning to fidget; looking for some exercise for that blade he was turning through his fingers. Looking Bud's way as if he was all set to —

Nobody had heard so much as an insect's buzz out there in the night; nobody suspected there might be a prowler moving silently, stealthily round the post, waiting his chance to edge closer, come to within a few feet of the window that gave a clear view of the four men seated at the table. And nobody had the slightest notion of the prowler's rifle barrel levelling on its target, the hatred that eased to a glint of coldly calculated destruction in the man's eyes, the finger that took the first pressure at the trigger. But everybody heard the roar of the shot that shattered the night like a demon's snarl.

Mitch Siers took the blast full in the throat and was thrown back from the table in a flying spray of blood and flailing limbs. Lobo brushed the whiskey bottle to the floor, came to his feet and crashed against the wall. Jensen sat open-mouthed, hands tight in their grip on an empty glass, the sweat glistening on his face. Monaghan was at the door and flinging it open in an instant, his Colt already blazing wildly into the night.

But Bud Ziggers did not move save to murmur the same word over and over again until the name 'Ocachi' seemed to fill the gloom like a haunting echo.

4

'He'll die — die like a dog — and I'll be doing the killin'.' Rufus Lobo glared into the black silent night as if seeing beyond it, without so much as a twitch through his bulk, without seeming to breathe or blink or be aware of those gathered in the shadowy lantern glow at his back; with his blood coursing through his veins like a surge of angry lava. 'Yuh hear me?' he hissed a full minute later. 'Yuh hearin' me loud and clear?'

'We hear yuh,' chimed Monaghan, scuffing a boot slowly through the dirt. 'And we'll be with yuh, rest on that. We'll see Mitch avenged for whoever it was fired that shot.'

'Damnit, I know who fired that shot!' snarled Lobo, turning to settle his bloodshot gaze on Monaghan. 'That 'breed — the one they call Ocachi.'

Bud Ziggers shivered. Fellow was right about that, he thought. Siers's death had been Ocachi's doing, sure enough, and maybe he would not be the last, not after what these sonsofbitches had done.

'So what's yuh thinkin'?' drawled Jensen, folding his arms.

'Thinkin'? T'ain't *thinkin'* that's needed,' snapped Lobo. 'It's doin', f'Crissake, and there's only one kinda doin' I got in mind — gettin' out there, findin' that 'breed and killin' him, real slow, so that he knows who's doin' it and why.'

Jensen grunted. 'Much the same as he's plannin'.'

'And what the hell's that supposed to mean?' growled Lobo.

'Plain enough,' shrugged Jensen. 'Fella comes back to find his woman in the state we left that squaw ain't takin' it lyin' down, is he, 'breed or no 'breed?'

'Yuh sayin' what I think yuh sayin'?' said Lobo, his eyes narrowing to dark slits. 'That *he* plans on killin' *us*?'

'No less,' shrugged Jensen again. 'Nature of the fella, ain't it?'

Lobo took a step forward. 'Nature, eh, that what yuh call it? Well, let me tell yuh about nature. See that boy sprawled in his own blood back there, dead as he's ever goin' to get; yuh see that? I raised him, took him from nothin', treated him like my own. He was about all I had. Yeah, all I had ... Well, nobody ain't takin' Mitch from me without payin', high as it goes, all the way. Now that's what I figure for nature.'

'My feelin's exactly,' nodded Monaghan. 'We'll go get the sonofabitch 'breed soon as it's light.'

'And where yuh goin' to find him?' asked Jensen. 'Yuh don't figure for him sittin' in that burned-out cabin waitin' on yuh, do yuh?'

'Don't give a spit where he is,' growled Lobo. 'We find him. Long as it takes. Yuh with us, Joe?'

Jensen unfolded his arms and hooked

his thumbs in his belt. 'Been with yuh long enough, may as well see it through,' he drawled.

'Yuh make it sound a deal final,' said Lobo.

' 'Breed up front waitin' on yuh; marshal trailin' in at yuh back. Odds look a mite stacked from here. Still . . . ' Jensen shrugged again and turned to the veranda. 'Meantime, we got a body to bury.'

Lobo spat defiantly. 'Mebbe we should've kept ridin'. Just kept goin'.'

'Yeah,' said Jensen, moving away. 'Mebbe we should at that.'

★ ★ ★

They dug a deep grave for Mitch Siers and had laid him to rest long before sun-up. Only then, when Lobo had settled his hat firmly back on his head, did the three men turn their attention to Bud Ziggers.

'What we goin' to do about him?' asked Monaghan, sliding a slow, hungry glance over Bud. 'Want me to finish him?'

'He comes with us,' murmured Lobo. 'I gotta job for him.'

'Hell, Rufus,' frowned Monaghan, 'what we want with a played-out, tradin'-post critter? I don't see no use for him.'

'That's 'cus yuh never get to usin' what few brains yuh got!' scowled Lobo. 'He knows this Ocachi fella, don't he, knows his thinkin', where he'll head, what he'll do. That so, yuh old buzzard?'

Bud swallowed, sweated, fumbled for his corn-cob pipe. 'I ain't doin' nothin' — '

'So yuh want Clips here to go givin' that blade of his some exercise?' said Lobo. 'Believe me, fella, he's just frettin' on that, and he won't be in no hurry neither. Now, yuh goin' to do like I say, or let Monaghan rearrange yuh miserable face? Choice is yours.'

'Yuh'll get put to hell one of these days,' croaked Bud, wiping at the sweat.

'Yeah, yeah, I been hearin' that all my life. Yuh just go cover them trappers' bodies, scatter their mounts and put t'gether some supplies. Clips, yuh go with him. We're pullin' out in an hour.'

Lobo turned at the sound of Jensen's boot scuffing the dirt. 'What's with you? Still listenin' out for that marshal?'

'Mebbe,' drawled Jensen, 'but I guess he'll figure things for himself once he gets here.'

Lobo spat and sighed. 'Darn me if yuh don't take some reckonin', Joe Jensen. Yuh just go on and on scratchin' away like yuh were porch-perchin' on a flea bag. I told yuh once, I'll tell yuh again — '

'I hear yuh,' said Jensen, 'and I ain't backin' off. We'll ride like yuh say, go chasin' this 'breed, but just yuh keep turnin' round, Rufus, watchin' for what's comin' up.'

'I'll do that,' snapped Lobo. 'Make sure yuh heed yuh own words.'

'Oh, I will,' grinned Jensen. 'Yuh can bet yuh life on it.'

★ ★ ★

They trailed out of the trading post for the foothills of the Moccasins at the first crease of light, Lobo heading up the party, Bud Ziggers close at his side. Jensen, Monaghan and a packhorse followed some distance back, neither man caring to say a deal, both indulging Lobo as they always had by going along with his thinking.

The loss of Mitch Siers was of no great concern to Monaghan. He had never taken to the youth, anyhow, and always reckoned Lobo had given him far more attention and protection than was good for him. Siers should have stood to his own patch, not had Lobo sweeten it for him.

But what did bother Monaghan was the manner of Siers's death. That 'breed had stalked around the trading post like an animal, intent on only one thing: killing any one of the four men at the table. Mitch had drawn the short straw. And now Lobo had reacted exactly as Ocachi had reckoned — set out to hunt him down. What Lobo seemed not to be rating was that the hunt would be on the 'breed's terms, on his ground. That, Monaghan thought, smacked of real danger, with the odds weighed heavily on one side. Fellow never went in search of odds stacked like that, not if he wanted to stay breathing.

Joe Jensen was a deal more troubled, and for different reasons.

Jensen had been against the ride into Bitters, against stopping at the cabin and taking the squaw woman like they had, and staying on to liquor up at the post would not have rated a priority in his thinking — not if they wanted to keep putting the miles between themselves and Marshal Randall. And it was Randall, he figured, they should be bothering about. He was not going to let go the scent he had clear on his nostrils. He liked it, wanted more and was all set to get it. And meantime, there was the 'breed . . . Only thing he wanted was to avenge the death of his woman, and at any price.

Seemed to Jensen as if Lobo had bitten off all he could chew in one take, and the 'meat' either way you looked at it was personal.

Bud Ziggers was sure as hell troubled, through every pore, in every muscle, creaking at every bone. And it all looked set to stay that way. Sure, he could ride here at Lobo's side and tell him what he knew of the hills and mountains and where Ocachi *might* be, what he *might* do — but never when or how. And first time his reckoning proved wrong . . . End of Bud Ziggers! Only consolation in that lay in being free of that flea-mangy mattress back there at the post.

But maybe there was a splinter of hope. That marshal these scumbags went on about — who was he, where had he come from, why was he on their tails, and how come he seemed to bother that fellow Jensen so much? Must be some marshal . . . more to the point, where was he right now?

Not up there, thought Bud, scanning the folds of the hills to the mountain range, but somebody was; somebody who had lit a fire and had no fear of the smoke being seen. Or somebody who planned on just that.

5

'What yuh make of that?' growled Lobo, watching the column of smoke. 'Yuh figure that's him?' He tugged at the reins of Ziggers's mount. 'Well, I'm askin' yuh, fella — who the hell's up there?'

'Could be him,' croaked Bud, blinking furiously. 'Could be Ocachi. Ain't no real tellin'.'

'That ain't no stalkin' 'breed's fire,' said Monaghan, reining close by. 'He ain't goin' to make it that easy, is he? No, I figure that for trappers.'

Lobo spat into the dirt. 'I've had my fill of trappers, but I don't want any hereabouts 'til this business is done. Trappers get under yuh feet. Let's go settle them.'

'I'm for that,' grinned Monaghan. 'And this early in the day, too!'

'Time wastin',' called Jensen from

down the track. 'What yuh wanna waste time with them for?'

' 'Cus they're there, damnit, that's why!' snapped Lobo. 'I swear, Joe, I get to wonderin' sometimes if yuh losin' yuh nerve.'

Jensen merely shrugged. 'Have it your way.'

'Come on now, Joe,' smiled Monaghan. 'Let's go have ourselves some fun. And I bet the coffee's simmerin' at that!'

The four men reined away to the right and began the slow haul to the higher ground and the spiralling column of smoke. Hell, thought Bud, supposing it was Ocachi up there? Would he really have made it that obvious? Not like him, not when he could go soft as a breeze, darn near invisible. Or was it trappers? He would reckon not; they were too high, in too much open ground. Any trapper worth his pants stayed lower and closer to the pines. Could be that marshal, of course . . .

'Ain't in no hurry to show themselves, are they?' clipped Monaghan, already fingering the butt of his Colt. 'Lazy critters!'

'Move up ahead, Clips,' ordered Lobo. 'See how many we're dealin' with — and don't get hoggin' 'em all for y'self!'

Monaghan went ahead at a steady trot, weaving between the bulge and reach of massed boulders until he was out of sight and there was only the sound of hoofs clipping rock.

'Can't be more than a couple of 'em,' murmured Lobo. 'Yuh reckon so, old man?'

Bud swallowed nervously. 'Trappers ain't usually this high. Tend to stay lower, but that ain't to say — '

'I'd reckon on the 'breed watchin' us right now,' said Jenson drawing level with the packhorse. 'I'd wager a hundred dollars he's up there somewhere, tight in the run to them peaks.'

Lobo's gaze scanned the sprawl of the mountains. 'Yuh mean he's been eyein' us since we left the post?'

'Well, he ain't been sewin' buttons on his shirt, has he?' drawled Jensen. 'If he wants us out here — and we've sure as hell obliged him — he wants us here on his terms, always in his sight. Wouldn't you?'

Lobo flashed an angry glance. 'Mebbe. All depends — '

'Mebbe nothin'!' snapped Jensen. 'He knows this country, every twitch and turn of it. Hell, Rufus, he can lead us just where he wants!'

'*Thinks* he can,' grinned Lobo. 'He's a sonofabitch and he ain't walkin' clear of killin' Mitch, not while I'm still breathin'.'

'And he feels just the same about levellin' up for that squaw of his,' said Jensen, half-turning in his saddle to narrow his gaze on the track they had followed. 'We ain't got no company, not yet.'

Lobo hissed between his teeth. 'If I hear one more mention of that goddamn marshal . . . Hold it, Clips is comin' back.'

They watched Monaghan round the bulge of the boulders, his stare fixed and tight, hands loose on the reins. 'Yuh'd best come take a look,' he called through a cracked, brittle voice. 'If yuh got the stomach.'

★ ★ ★

The fire had burned to embers and ash, the smoke begun to swirl and cloud in a thickening grey shroud that hugged the bloodsoaked sand and stone surrounding it and drifted over the torn, ragged remnants of clothing. It looked to be a place of ritual, as if some sacrifice to an unknown god had been slaughtered here and left for whatever spirit it appeased to gloat over. A place of sudden and violent death that reeked now of blood, dead flame and smouldering cloth where nothing moved save the smoke.

'Them's the squaw's clothes,' croaked Lobo. 'The ones she was wearing.'

'But that ain't her blood,' murmured

Jensen. 'That's animal blood.'

'Don't matter a damn, does it?' said Monaghan, wiping the sweat from his face. 'It's the 'breed's doin'. Ocachi's been here, arranged all this for our benefit — just to remind us what we done.' The sweat trickled to his chin. 'He's been watchin' us all along, since we rode out.'

'Shut yuh whinin',' growled Lobo. 'This don't spook me none. Just goes to show we're closin' in on him. Damnit, he can't be far away.'

'Yuh call this 'closin' in'?' drawled Jensen. 'F'Crissake, Rufus, the 'breed's baitin' yuh! He's settin' yuh up.'

Lobo spat into the smear of blood. 'Nobody's settin' me up. Nobody, yuh hear?' he growled again. 'I ain't bein' led no dance by no 'breed. I figure for the sonofabitch bein' a spit away. We can get this over with before nightfall.' He swung round in the saddle to face Ziggers. 'So what yuh reckon, old fella? Where is he?'

'How the hell should I know?'

45

blurted Bud. 'Could be any one of a dozen places, mebbe lookin' yuh straight in the eye right now.'

Lobo lashed out to settle a sickening thud of boot into Ziggers's thigh. 'I ain't askin' yuh to speculate,' he yelled. 'I wanna know where the 'breed's holed up, damn yuh.'

'He don't know any more than you,' said Jensen, pushing his mount between the two men. 'Fella's right, 'breed could be anywhere. Yuh ain't goin' to know 'til yuh see him — and that might be too late.'

'Damn yuh, Joe — ' scowled Lobo.

'I'm for turnin' for that bank at North Forks,' called Monaghan, reining his mount tight. 'We ain't doin' no good here.'

'And what about Mitch?' snapped Lobo. 'He mean nothin' to yuh now, that the way of it?'

'Mitch's dead, and there ain't nothin' goin' to bring him back. I say North Forks before this 'breed gets any closer.' Monaghan brought his mount square on to Lobo. 'Bein' dead's the end of it, Rufus. Mitch ain't givin' a cuss either way now, is he?'

'First man who rides outa here is a dead man, I swear it,' growled Lobo. 'And that includes you, Clips. No messin'.'

Monaghan reined back. Bud Ziggers's mount bucked. The packhorse snorted.

'Gettin' to us already, ain't it?' said Jensen. 'Just like Ocachi wants it so's we don't trust nothin' and nobody, not even our own shadows. And we ain't no more than a few hours started.'

'We're goin' on,' croaked Lobo. 'And I ain't hearin' no other. 'Breed can do all he likes to spook us, much blood as he wants, but that's all it is — spookin' us — and spookin' ain't never — '

They each of them heard the zinging whine through the still, silent air; they might have seen the blur of the arrow as it sped like a shimmering flame through the light, but only one man felt the agony of it settling into the flesh and screamed at the searing rage of its heat.

Clips Monaghan fell from his mount with the arrow buried deep in his thigh and his warm blood oozing to the already stained, baked dirt.

6

Ocachi loped down the spread of rocks and boulders to the bed of the creek as if he had eyes in the soles of his feet. Never once did he slow his pace, lose his balance, pause for a moment to be sure of the ground ahead or shift his gaze from the trickling flow of bright water below him. His feet 'saw' their way and knew instinctively where to fall without disturbing so much as a pebble.

It was another full minute before he had reached the water and turned to where it ran deepest and coolest in the shade of a rock slab overhang. Only then did he halt, wait, listen for a moment for the slightest sound, and let his unusually blue piercing eyes scan the way he had come and the crawl of the creek beyond the shade. Here would do fine, he thought, lowering the bow and Winchester to the ground, then easing the quiver and skin water-bag from his broad, suntanned shoulders. Time to rest, gather his strength, let the heat of the high day pass and the shadows lengthen from the west.

Time, too, for the men trailing him to fathom his tracks and follow — just as he planned they should.

He drank carefully, watchfully from the creek, and when his thirst was sated, cupped the clear water over his naked chest and arms until it trickled cool and soft to stain his buckskin pants and boots. He closed his eyes for a moment to relish the satisfaction, licked his lips, then came slowly to his full height, stretched and rested his hands on his hips.

His breathing was easier now, the lift and fall of his powerful chest rhythmic and free for the first time in hours of the ache that had fluttered constantly at his heart. But he sighed even so in the sudden rush of images that flared and crowded through his thoughts: the burning cabin, the stench of flame and smoke, scorched furniture, clothes, the skins of bedding, the flesh of the foal that had been too slow, too scared to race with its mother from the corral and been roasted alive; the raging pockets of fire, scattered embers, blackened sand, timbers bereft of cladding that reached for the sky like the bones of petrified skeletons — and there, on what had remained of the floor of the cabin's main room, the abused and mutilated body of his wife, her round brown eyes fixed in the final moment of agony, terror and death.

The sigh drifted on and he was back again with the heat of his sweat, the thundering beat in his head as he had ridden that night in search of the men who had crushed his world to cold dust; found them at Ziggers's trading post, listened to their whiskey-sodden talk, shot the young one seated at the table, and vowed then, when he had finally stood alone in the mountains with the last of the fire smoke curling to the moon and the words of Red Eye clear in his thoughts, that the three he had left alive would die at his hand, in his way, in his time.

He blinked, listened, then turned to the deeper shade of the overhang. Two hours, perhaps three, he thought, before the men following would plan to settle for the night. The one he had wounded would slow them up, so that they would reach only as far as the last of the pines where the narrower, one-horse tracks began their twisting climb to the hills. Good. It would be there that he would strike again. There, when the moon was high above the peaks of the Moccasin range.

Ocachi squatted, his gaze unmoving on the flow of the creek stream, stray shafts of light shimmering on his black shoulder-length hair, and cleared his mind of the painful images until he was alone with only the spirit of Red Eye.

'You are Ocachi,' the chief had said all those years ago, 'born of two bloods, who will grow to know the pain and dreams of both, hear the words of the Comanche and share the thoughts of the white man, run the paths of one, ride the trails of the other, walk with light and see the darkness, and in the darkness see the light, listen to two truths, fathom the lies in each, be at my side and those of your Comanche brothers, but pass in the shadows of white chiefs and be at ease. Two worlds you must learn to know and understand, and where there is the need, find strength to choose for what you see is right. This will be the mark of Ocachi.'

'As you say,' murmured Ocachi to the echo of his memories, and closed his eyes as the images and hatred flooded back.

* * *

Marshal Jim Randall had neither the inclination nor stomach for a breakfast of any kind, save what he might find in the dregs of his whiskey flask, and maybe it would be admitting a weakness to indulge this early. Better, he figured, to get the hell out of this place and push on to the foothills, take in some clean, fresh air.

He grunted, wiped a hand over the icy sweat on his face and reined his mount clear of the ash and embers of the burned-out cabin. The horse snorted against the sudden stench of rotting flesh and tossed its head at the tightening rein. 'Easy, boy, easy,' soothed Randall. 'Know how yuh feel.'

And he did too. Not a man living or a horse standing that would not be spooked at the evil here, and not a soul breathing who would leave without the company of ghosts. But when it came to asking whose hand it was had delved this low, Randall had all the answers: Rufus Lobo and his scumbag sidekicks, Clips Monaghan, Gentle Joe Jensen, Mitch Siers. But they had sure made some mistake after the mayhem reeked at Bitters in turning from the trail for the cabin!

Obvious now, thought Randall, easing the mount towards the foothills, that Lobo had never heard of the one-time scout, Ocachi, or that he had come to settle with his Comanche wife in the Moccasins. But just as obvious that he had sure as hell heard of him now, and felt the first heat of the revenge Ocachi would reap for the death of his woman. That much had been plain as day back there at the trading post when Randall had ridden in the previous night to find the place deserted save for the bodies of two dead trappers and the marker over Mitch Siers's grave.

Ocachi had struck, and fast.

Randall grunted quietly to himself as the mount settled to a gentle trot. Not much doubt now, he reckoned, that Lobo had gone in search of Ocachi and taken the old post manager, Bud Ziggers, with him. Another mistake! Siers had been like a son at Lobo's side for as long as the youngster had been riding with him, but taking up the hunt for Ocachi to avenge his death was about as deadly as juggling fire sticks with one hand tied behind you. Ocachi would almost certainly lure Lobo deep into the mountains, and when the time and place were right . . .

All a question now of who would get to Lobo and his sidekicks first — Ocachi or the law in the shape of Marshal Jim Randall.

Randall grunted again. It had taken a whole heap of long, hot, dusty days for him to get a sound lead on Lobo's whereabouts and settle to his trail; a time out of his life he could ill-afford at his age. So maybe he should call it a day right now, leave the sonofabitch to whatever fate awaited him up there in the mountains. But that would be turning his back on the vow he had made in the stain and stench of the bloodbath he had found at the homestead out of Passmore. Hank Cutler, his wife, their daughter, the three of them dead and abused at the hands of Lobo, just like it had been at Ocachi's cabin.

No lawman turned his back on that, however much the joints might get to creaking and the prospect of a warm bed come cold nights beckon. No, he never turned his back . . .

He raised a hand to shield his eyes against the early sun glare over the mountains. Five years and more since he had last trailed the Moccasins, he recalled. Ocachi had still been scouting out of Fort Warsash then, Bud Ziggers running a thriving trading post, and Randall chasing a bunch of bank robbers out of Devlin. Times sure had changed, and he never had got to them robbers.

But the mountains had. Only trace they ever found of the men was their boots. Not another thing. It was as if the deep black shadows that lay up there like open mouths had swallowed them.

Shadows had not changed one bit, he thought, riding on.

7

'Kill him now, or let him bleed to death. Comes to the same thing.' Lobo directed a long line of spittle into the flickering flames of the fire and waited until the sizzle had faded before lifting his dark gaze to Jensen's face. 'Yuh figure?' he grunted.

Joe Jensen stretched his long legs over the sand and eased back on his bedroll. 'Yuh'd do that?' he asked. 'Yuh'd shoot him?'

'Same as I would a lame horse,' said Lobo, wiping a hand across his mouth. 'Wouldn't you — or am I set to get one of them long sermons of yours?'

Jensen shrugged a shoulder. 'Shouldn't have gotten to this, should it? Shouldn't be here, should we? Shouldn't be doin' what we're doin', and Clips sure as hell shouldn't be sprawled out there with half an arrow buried in his thigh.'

'But we are, damnit, and he is!' snapped Lobo, his gaze darkening over the glow of the flames. 'Trouble with you, Joe, is yuh just never get to livin' in the real world. Always philosophizin' on what might have been, should've been, could've been. Hell, I sometimes reckon on yuh bein' just plain stuffed with 'mights' and 'beens!''

Jensen's eyes narrowed for a moment, then relaxed in a wide, lazy gaze over the night shroud settling through the mountains. 'We could make it to North Forks in a couple days. Get Clips to a doc. He might make it.'

'There yuh go again,' growled Lobo, 'Clips *might* make it. 'Course he ain't goin' to make it, not nowhere, not no-how. He's finished, not worth saddle space even if he did live. So there ain't no choices, are there?'

'So yuh goin' to kill him?'

'Sure, if that's the way of it.'

'And keep right on trackin' down that 'breed?'

'Too right,' grinned Lobo. ' 'Til I get to skinnin' the sonofabitch alive.'

'You're a fool,' murmured Jensen.

'Yuh reckon? Well, if yuh're goin' to be right alongside of me like yuh always are, that'll make you the joker, won't it?'

'Don't count on it,' said Jensen, lowering his gaze to the flames. 'Not permanent, anyhow.'

Lobo growled again and aimed another line of spittle to the fire.

* * *

He had that grey pinched look of a man listening out for death who had already heard it whisper. Bud Ziggers had seen it before; too many times in too many men; some not all bad and some bad enough. But when it came to Clips Monaghan, he just hoped the fellow heard the rattle loud and clear when it got close. Sooner the better in Bud's reckoning, and long before sun-up if that bleeding did not ease.

Even so, he thought, raising the canteen to Monaghan's lips again, there was a measure of some decency deserving of every man — sons-of-gunslinging-bitches included! Which was a deal more than Rufus Lobo was ready to consider. Hang it, that scumbag would as soon finish the job as look at the fellow, and he probably would if a dying man threatened his planning.

Bud grunted quietly to himself and glanced round the place they had come to hole up for the night: near to a bone-dry creek-bed foot of a sprawl of pine and rock that looked to be the dead-end of the track they had been following. An eerie, haunted place where a fellow seemed to be surrounded by the silence, where even his own breathing spooked. Not much hope of a deal of sleep here, he thought, and not that he would bother, not with Lobo in a frame of mind where he might do anything, and not with Ocachi lurking out there somewhere.

Bud swallowed on his gritty throat. Hell, would Ocachi hit again during the night, who would be his target this time? Jensen, or would he finish Monaghan? Not Lobo, not yet. He swallowed again. And what about that marshal? Supposing . . .

'He goin' to live?' croaked Lobo, his shadow bulging like a rolled rock over Bud and Monaghan.

Bud spat, came upright from his knees and stared hard into Lobo's face. 'T'ain't goin' to be no thanks to you if he does,' he grunted.

Lobo grinned. 'Gettin' a mite sassy, aren't we? Yuh figure yuh got some value round here? Reckon Joe and me can't be doin' without yuh? Well, forget it, old man. Yuh're breathin' on my say-so. Simple as that. So don't go reckonin' on a long future for y'self. Got it?' He slung his weight to one hip. 'Now, he goin' to live, or ain't he?'

'Losin' too much blood,' said Bud. 'Can't plug it no how. And he's fevered up fit to melt. If that arrowhead ain't lifted from his thigh . . . he won't see t'morrow's noon. Meantime, if Ocachi gets — '

Lobo's fist smashed into Bud's face with all the lightning speed of a thunderbolt. 'Yuh don't mouth nothin' of that 'breed, til I ask, yuh understand?' he growled, grabbing Bud by the collar of his shirt. 'Not one word.' The sweat on Lobo's brow was suddenly white and gleaming in the gloom. 'If Clips there ain't goin' to live, yuh go easy on the water. No wastin' it where it ain't doin' no good.'

Lobo had already turned and walked back to Jensen and the flickering glow of the fire, when Bud heard the sound somewhere deep in the sprawl of pines. A footfall; animal or human? Mountain lion out for supper, or somebody watching from up there? He glanced quickly at the two men seated at the fire; they had heard nothing. Good, thought Bud, kneeling again at Monaghan's side, let them just rest easy there, let them think the night was empty.

Give Ocachi all the space and time he needed.

★ ★ ★

Ocachi watched the beetle wait without moving on the broad, dusty leaf. The beetle knew he was there, could see him, sense him and feel the threat of danger, but knew too the wisdom of not moving too soon, too quickly, that survival depended on timing. So you must be patient, little fellow, thought Ocachi, wait for the danger to pass or know the moment for escape.

He shifted his gaze from the beetle to the window of space in the curtain of pines that gave him a clear view of the drift to the creek-bed, the glow of the fire, the men seated there and, set apart, the man he had wounded being tended by Ziggers. His lips flickered through a soft smile; Ziggers was one of true compassion who, even now, would not leave a man to die alone. But the man would die, perhaps before sunup.

Ocachi's smile faded as his gaze shifted again, this time to the deeper shadows and the men's line-hitched mounts. He noted and examined each one; four and the packhorse. Two from five would leave three, enough for Lobo, Jensen and Ziggers to move on at first light.

So be it. They would take the safe track out of the creek to the place where the red hawks nested; only then would they have to choose between going higher or tracking to the lower reaches. He would make certain they went higher.

Ocachi grunted softly, flexed his fingers and slid them to the handle of the knife at his belt. He glanced at the blade and grunted again. Soon its edge would have better things to do than cut the rope of a hitch-line. Soon.

The beetle waited until Ocachi had crept away before moving to a darker, lower leaf. The danger, it sensed, had not gone far.

8

It was a noise a deal more decisive than the shifting of a beetle that disturbed Marshal Randall from his sleep in the rock cleft. He was awake, wide-eyed and holding his breath at the first crack of twig — not that he could see a thing in the deep hugging darkness of the night, nothing that might put a shape to the sound that had been only yards away.

He waited, listening, not daring to move save to slide his fingers to the butt of his Colt. Ten seconds, twenty, a full minute passed before he heard it again; another crack, a muffled swish of pine branches, the dull thud of steps over dirt and dried earth. Hoofs, horses being coaxed, eased gently into frightening darkness, but not afraid, confident in the one who led them.

Randall eased his body from the

cleft, winced at the stab of pain in his back, and peered hard into the night to where he had hitched his mount. The mare stood stiff and erect, neck tensed, ears pricked, eyes round and bright, but she stayed silent.

Keep it that way, he thought, coming fully upright, waiting a moment, listening, then slipping after the sound like an animal stalking its prey.

He moved a single, cautious step at a time, judging the distance between himself and the sound, holding always a few yards short of it; pausing, waiting, moving on, certain that somebody up ahead was going to a hell of a deal of trouble to shift his mounts — and in the middle of the night at that.

So who might it be who was slipping through the shadows as if one of them, who seemed to know the drift of the ground as well as he did the palm of his own hand? Who could coax the trust of horses to see and feel no danger in the dark? Only one man he would figure for that: Ocachi. But whose horses was he moving, where to, and why? And if —

That was as far as Randall's pondering went as the swishing, slithering sounds ahead faded to an echo and he was suddenly, violently, into a crashing spin and fall.

Something thick and heavy thudded across his shoulders felling him to a sprawling lunge over dirt, stone, pine needles and spiky growth. He groaned, winced, came to a shuddering halt against a rotting tree branch, blinked and was clambering round on his knees to face whoever it was had bushwhacked him when he was struck again, this time across the head, skimming a daze of stars over the darkness and a stabbing pain that pierced the length of his body.

And then there were no more sounds for Marshal Randall on that night.

★　★　★

'He what I think he is?' said the toothless man, slapping his lips over soft, dripping gums. 'We got ourselves a lawman? We done that?'

'We done that, Blooney,' grunted his bearded, one-eyed partner adjusting the patch over his blind eye. 'Done it, and no mistake. Now ain't that somethin'?' He peered closer at the man sprawled unconscious in the scuffed mass of pine cones and needles. 'Yuh figure it's somethin'?'

'I ain't sure, Salts,' murmured Blooney, wiping a hand across his mouth. 'I ain't sure at all. A lawman . . . We ain't never had ourselves a lawman before. And out here at that, with all this comin' and goin'. No, I just ain't sure. Yuh sure?'

'Sure I'm sure,' grinned Salts. 'Yuh just ain't reckonin' proper, are yuh? Ain't seein' it.'

'Ain't I?'

'No, yuh ain't, nothin' like. So I'll reckon it for yuh, shall I? Make it simple so's yuh understand, eh?'

'Yuh do that, Salts,' said Blooney, still watching the seemingly lifeless body.

'I'm for listenin' to yuh.'

'Good.' Salts adjusted his eye-patch again and winged a line of spittle into the night. 'So here's the way of it. How long we been up here in these mountains — five months, six? And what we got for the trouble? Nothin', save some old boots meat just enough to live on, eh? That the size of it?'

'Right,' said Blooney. ' 'S'right. Old boots meat — and blisters size of cackle-berries.'

'Them too. Then our luck shifts, don't it? Sure it does. And here's how. First we see that Ocachi fella hot-footin' it up here like he had a scorched butt. Why ain't our concern, so we don't mess. Right? Right. Then, glory be, who's next? Nobody less than Rufus Lobo himself, that sonofabitch Mon-aghan, Gentle Joe *and* Bud Ziggers. Now why Ziggers, and why, my friend, ain't Mitch Siers with Lobo?'

'No knowin',' blinked Blooney.

'I'll tell yuh why — 'cus Siers is dead. Dead, and mebbe that Indian scout is the cause of it. Yuh figure?'

Blooney blinked again. 'Nope, not like yuh doin'.'

'Well, I do,' grunted Salts. 'But that ain't all, is it, not the top and bottom of it? Nossir. Next thing we know we got this lawman here high-tailin' it into the hills. Now what in tarnation is he doin' here, and why is it that half the territory is suddenly beatin' it into the Moccasins like somebody had turned stone into gold? Tell me that, will yuh?'

'Can't,' grunted Blooney.

''Cus yuh ain't figurin'. 'S'clear enough when you piece it together. Lobo is trackin' Ocachi, the lawman is trailin' Lobo.'

'Say, that could be the way of it,' grinned Blooney.

'That it is, and we, Blooney, sure as yuh stinkin' socks, are holdin' the full deck in this trackin' game. We're dealin'; y'self and me — us!'

'How's that?' frowned Blooney.

''Cus we got the lawman, ain't we, and Lobo's goin' to be real grateful

— *real grateful* — for that, bet yuh boots.' Salts' one eye gleamed as it settled like a light on the body. 'Lobo'll pay handsome for gettin' his hands on this fella. Oh, yes . . . Get his hands on him and get him off his back while he goes stalkin' that 'breed — and fillin' our pockets into the bargain, enough for us to get the hell out of these mountains and go find ourselves some soft-belly livin'. Yuh with me, Blooney?'

Blooney slapped his sodden lips. 'Well . . . ' he began, 'I kinda see it, but there ain't no guarantee Lobo's goin' to pay up, is there? He ain't exactly got a reputation for holdin' to his word, has he? And another thing — '

'Darn me, Blooney, if yuh ain't gettin' to be one helluva pumpkin roller in yuh old age! Complainin' one minute, jiggin' like a frayed nerve the next! Don't yuh never see a silver linin' when it slaps yuh in the eyes?'

''Course I do. All I'm sayin' is — '

'Yuh said enough,' snapped Salts. 'We get this fella trussed and on our way, go

72

find Lobo. He won't be far away. Somewhere along the creek-bed, I'd reckon.'

'And what about Ocachi?' asked Blooney. 'What we do about him?'

'Nothin',' smiled Salts. 'Don't have to, do we? No need. We seen him leadin' them two mounts out, didn't we, not an hour back? Lobo's horses, sure to be. And that's another reason for Lobo clappin' welcomin' eyes on us, ain't it? He's goin' to want all the guns he can lay his hands on to get even with that 'breed scout.'

'Us?' frowned Blooney, slapping his lips again. 'You and me? Guns for Lobo?'

'Sure, and why not? Yuh gotta gun, ain't yuh? Yuh can shoot, can't yuh? Hell, Blooney, just how much spellin' out do yuh need?'

'A whole lot if I'm linin' m'self alongside Rufus Lobo and the likes of his outfit. I heard tell as how — '

'Yuh heard too much and said all yuh goin' to say if you and me are stayin' partners.' Salts pushed irritably at his eye-patch. 'Now let's move it, shall we?'

'But I ain't got no argument with Ocachi. What the hell I wanna go shootin' him up for?'

''Cus yuh want dollars in yuh pocket, steak in yuh belly and a warm woman in yuh bed, that's why. Now, will yuh move it, f'Crissake?'

Blooney grunted, blinked and stared long and hard into the deep night as if suddenly aware it had been watching them.

★ ★ ★

Ocachi fondled the noses of the two mounts he held in the darkest shadows of a close-standing clutch of pines, murmured to them through a soft, low hum, but held his gaze steady on the space beyond the trees.

The trappers he had been aware of since nightfall, had stalked the lone man and taken their prey. Now they talked of handing him to Lobo — so the man was of value, someone Lobo wished to hold prisoner, or kill more like. A lawman, trailing the gunslingers; a man with a score to settle. This Lobo had many enemies, perhaps more than he could handle. But what of the lawman, he wondered? Should he leave him with the trappers, wait until they joined up with Lobo? What would be the white-man's thinking? How would Comanche fathom the choice?

Ocachi's gaze shifted to settle on the wild blaze of confusion in the eyes of the horses. Soon, at the approach of light, he would hide them deep in the foothills in readiness for the day they would be needed.

9

Say what you like, look at it any way you cared, this was a killer. And it was as certain as sundown that it was going to do just that — kill him! Bud Ziggers stumbled again, winced as the rope binding his wrists tightened under Jensen's tug, and wondered for the hundredth time that morning how long it would be before he finally fell face-down in the dirt and was either hauled to his death or cut free and tossed into the teeth of that hungry creek down there.

Damn it, this was no way for a fellow to end his days, no way at all, and from where he was seeing things right now, there was going to be precious little chance of coming out of it. Nothing, leastways, short of a miracle, and they, he reckoned, were in short supply out here. Fact was, too, that things were getting worse. Figure it. . .

Monaghan was still alive, just, but more dead than breathing slumped there in the saddle just back of Lobo, and Lobo was a deal more sweated up and fuming than he had been the night before. It had been the loss of the horses that had torched his anger. Or was it the fact that Ocachi had slid like a shadow to the hitch-line and snitched those mounts from right under Lobo's nose, easy as lifting eggs from a dozy hen? Hell, that had riled him!

All that had been bad enough, but gotten worse when those scumbag trappers, Blooney and Salts, had ridden in close on sun-up with that lawman, Randall, nursing a sore head and with a look on his face fit to scare a rattler out of its skin.

Jensen had smiled a 'told yuh so' smile that had stabbed real deep into Lobo's pride, and he might have come to shooting the marshal there and then had Salts not stepped in to talk of holding Randall as 'an ace' against

Ocachi making another strike.

'Reckon it,' the one-eyed trapper had grinned slyly, 'that 'breed ain't goin' to risk a hit that might, just might, do for the marshal here, is he? Nossir, t'aint in the 'breed's nature. And then yuh got the tradin'-post fella. Him and the marshal are yuh free passage, Mister Lobo, for just as long as yuh care to use 'em — 'til, in fact, yuh got Ocachi where you want him and can finish him at yuh will. Then, o' course, yuh can do as yuh wish with your hostage baggage. Have y'self some fun.' Salts' grin had broadened. 'And for a suitable consideration, m'self and my partner here'd be more than happy to place our catch at yuh disposal — if yuh get my meanin'?'

Lobo had stood sullen and silent for a whole minute before saying a word. He had stared like a vulture at Blooney and Salts — Blooney slapping his lips, Salts fidgeting with his eye-patch — then glanced at Bud, Monaghan, and searched Jensen's face as if looking into a mirror. His answer, such as it was, had been a grunt ahead of a sudden glint in his eyes.

Blooney and Salts had been bagged without a word mouthed, and they were just about dumb enough to figure Lobo for a fellow who stood to a deal!

Things had happened fast after that.

Monaghan, still bleeding and no more now than a blood-soaked heap of rags, had been loaded up on Bud's mount to trail a head behind Lobo; then came Blooney, Salts and Randall — the marshal trussed tight in the saddle — and finally Jensen dragging Bud at the end of a rope.

As mangy a troop of empty heads as you could wish to see, Bud had reckoned.

There had been no doubt about the track to follow — Ocachi had left it clear as warts on the palm of a hand — and Lobo had taken to it with barely a second glance, as blind as a bat, Bud had figured, to the fact that Ocachi was leading them higher and deeper in the

Moccasins, and well beyond the creek-bed and probably the only source of water for miles.

Could be, Bud had thought, that the prospect did not sit easy with Jensen. He had paid particular attention to the food and water they had been able to load up, but gazed more than once into those high, foreboding peaks and the deep shadowed lands that lay below them with a look of real doubt in his eyes. Just how long was Jensen prepared to pander to Lobo's obsession with revenge, and how far into the mountains would he trail before . . .

Before what? wondered Bud, watching the fellow now from the end of the rope; before Lobo exasperated him beyond patience, or before that marshal came back to his senses and got troublesome? Jensen seemed to rate Randall a higher priority than he did Ocachi.

Monaghan was already living on borrowed time and would be lucky to see noon. Lobo's accommodation of him was about all through. As for

Blooney and Salts, riding up there like they had panned pure gold out of coffee dregs, they were doomed fools and might just as well get to reckoning right now on how many more times they would blink.

As for Ocachi what about him, pondered Bud? No doubting where he was — loping along that daybreak skyline like some smooth, sleek animal on the hunt; watching them, plotting their every move, figuring on just when he would strike next. Blooney's and Salts' account on how they had seen Ocachi with the stolen mounts had served only to pinpoint where he had been hours back. This, mused Bud, was a new day, and with it would come a whole new deck of cards — with only one dealer. But just when and where would he deal?

A whole lot sooner and closer than anybody had reckoned, thought Bud, minutes later as he stumbled under another tug of the rope. Jensen's impatience had thrown Bud far to the right of the track, to a cleft between boulders, where, for just seconds, he had seen the shape of the figure high above him silhouetted against the morning glow.

Ocachi, poised there on all-fours like a mountain lion, just out of sight of the riders on the track but with a clear view of how many they were and where they were heading.

For a moment Bud was tempted to call out, but no point, he thought, and especially not now Jensen had reined up and was glaring back at him like he was all set to rid himself of his burden.

'I ain't fussed none whether yuh walk or get y'self dragged to wherever we're headin',' croaked Jensen. 'Choice is yours, mister.'

Bud pushed himself clear of the cleft, gripped the rope to hold his balance and was back on the track when a commotion up ahead drew Jensen's attention.

Monaghan had slid unconscious from the saddle and was sprawled on the track in a thickening pool of his own blood, Lobo staring down at him from his mount. 'He needs help,' spluttered Blooney. 'Needs a doc real fast.'

'Sure he does,' snapped Lobo, 'so mebbe yuh'd like to go rustle one up outa them rocks there.'

Blooney's eyes rounded until the whites gleamed. 'Now hold hard there, fella,' he spluttered again, 'yuh just can't go dealin' a hand like that. Mebbe one of us could get him outa here. Must be some place we could get some help.'

'Only one place Clips is goin',' drawled Lobo, 'and mighty pleased he'll be to see it.'

Lobo drew his Colt and shot Monaghan clean through the head almost before Blooney swallowed, before Salts blinked his one good eye, Randall opened either of his, and before Jensen and Bud Ziggers so much as twitched.

There were seconds then when only the drifting echo of the shot broke the silence, when no one moved or seemed to breathe, when smoke curled like a bewildered stray and the smell of cordite lingered on it.

'Best thing for him,' murmured Lobo, holstering the Colt.

'Hell,' croaked Blooney.

'Get that,' groaned Salts, fingering his eye-patch.

'Another hand to the 'breed,' muttered Jensen, slackening the rope to Ziggers.

Bud's eyes narrowed through a surge of sweat. No silhouetted shape on the rocks above him now, no sounds, no movements. Mountains might have been empty; there might not be a thing up there worth the noticing.

And then the arrow thudded into the dirt at the feet of Lobo's mount, the horse rose on its hindlegs as if baited with a hot poker, and the rider crashed to the ground with his hands flat in the pools of Clips Monaghan's blood.

10

'Get a hold on the mounts!' yelled Jensen above the clatter of hoofs, snorts and whinnying of the spooked mounts, shouts and croaked curses of men.

'Get the 'breed, damn yuh!' roared Lobo, scrambling on all-fours through the dirt and blood. 'Get him, yuh hear? Get him!'

'Get the hell out, more like!' spluttered Blooney.

'Damn it, get y'self into cover if yuh wanna stay alive,' called Salts, grabbing Blooney by the collar as he slid from his mount.

Randall was toppled from his horse, hands still tied, and rolled into the shelter of the boulders flanking the track. Jensen grabbed wildly, and uselessly, for flying reins. Ziggers felt the rope go slack, heaved, and fell back into a sprawl of rocks.

'Don't nobody think of runnin',' roared Lobo. 'First man who does is a dead man, I swear to God he is!'

'Get off the track!' screamed Jensen through the din and mayhem. ''Breed can take any one of yuh if yuh stay in the open.'

Randall tugged in vain at the rope binding his wrists. Ziggers did the same to the rope trussing him, and got nowhere. Jensen cursed as the freed mounts scattered in their panic, and now Lobo was on his feet again, his Colt blazing blindly into the hills.

'Save yuh lead!' shouted Jensen. 'There ain't nothin' to shoot at, damn yuh! Get the horses!'

Lobo swung round, his body tensed, eyes gleaming, sweat dripping, the Colt levelled to blaze at the first body seen running. But now Blooney and Salts were flat on their stomachs in the shadow of an overhang, Randall still in the boulders, Ziggers tight in the rocks, and only Jensen still mounted, fighting to control his bucking horse as he scanned the higher ground.

Lobo slipped in Monaghan's blood and skidded to his backside as a second arrow winged inches clear of his shoulder and buried itself in the swirling dirt surrounding Jensen.

There were seconds then when Jensen's mount grew in the dirt-cloud like a yellow-eyed spectre, seconds when he battled to stay in the saddle, hold to the reins, cursed, yelled a stream of incoherent abuse, lost his grip, felt himself thrown high as if caught in some freak twist of wind and hurled to the far side of the track where he lay conscious of only the sweat bubbling on his face, a stabbing pain in his back, and the sound of hoofbeats fading to a distant emptying echo.

* * *

'To hell with the sonofabitch!' croaked Lobo, flinging a rock into the blaze of sunlight, kicking at dirt, then spitting over a flat-faced stone. 'To hell with him! But he ain't got the better of things yet, not by a long shot he ain't. No way, and that's the size of it.'

'Size of it don't look good from where I'm sittin',' muttered Blooney, running a hand over his wet lips.

Salts nudged him and looked anxiously at Lobo. 'He don't mean it, Mister Lobo,' he grinned, 'not a word of it. Don't take no notice. We'll get that 'breed, see if we don't.'

Lobo spat again and glared at Jensen. 'We got a horse among us?' he asked.

'Nope, not one,' drawled Jensen, leaning back against the bulge of a boulder. 'So that settles it, I reckon.'

'What yuh mean, *settles* it?' croaked Lobo.

Jensen squinted against the sun blaze. 'We pull out, simple as that. And we do it while we got the chance. Get back to the tradin' post, see if we can rustle up a coupla horses — then ride like the wind outa this godforsaken hole.'

'That yuh figurin'?' said Lobo.

'That's my figurin', straight up, and it's yours too if yuh gotta grain of a brain. Don't make no sense to stay up here without horses, without food, and no water. That 'breed fella's holdin' the full deck, so we'd best scoot before he gets to playin' again. Pull out at sundown, keep goin' all night. We'll be into the foothills come first light.'

'Ocachi'll follow, yuh can bet,' murmured Ziggers.

'Sure he will,' said Jensen, 'but we take our chances, don't we? Odds shorten a deal by night, and we might get lucky.'

'I'm for that,' said Blooney, slapping his lips. 'Yep, that's for me.'

'Now yuh just hold it there, Blooney' croaked Salts, his one eye still on Lobo. 'Don't yuh go makin' no hasty decisions. We gotta deal to think on. This lawman here for one.'

Randall shifted in the shade of the overhang and pulled at the rope still binding his hands. 'Yep, yuh got me,' he mouthed cynically.

Lobo spat again. 'For just as long as I say so,' he said. 'And don't yuh go f'gettin' it, Lawman.'

Randall's gaze darkened, but he stayed silent.

'S'right, Mister Lobo,' smiled Salts, 'for just as long as yuh say, and that's a fact. Now, way I figure it — '

'Ain't interested in your figurin', mister,' snapped Jensen. 'I'd as soon shoot yuh now as later. I ain't fussed.'

Salts began to sweat, Blooney grinned, Lobo laughed and scratched his belly. 'Well, now, ain't we just a merry band, eh?' he smiled. 'Outa horses, outa food, outa water — and darn near outa guts!' His smile faded under a threatening scowl. 'Now yuh just hear me good, all of yuh. I lost Mitch and done the decent thing by Clips, but that's as far as the 'breed's meddlin' goes. He's had all he's gettin', yuh understand? No more. We're goin' on, right now. We're goin' to grab this Ocachi and he's goin' to die. Oh, yes, he's goin' to die. No messin'. And I

90

ain't steppin' outa these mountains 'til it's done — and neither are you, not one of yuh.'

Lobo drew his Colt and fanned it menacingly over the stares settled on him. 'And that's *my* figurin'.'

* * *

Ocachi tightened the knot, checked the tension in the rope, added a last touch to the covering hiding it, and stepped back to the shadows. He grunted a note of satisfaction as his blue eyes flashed. It was good, as he had planned. Now he had only to wait.

He slipped deeper into the shade between the rocks, moistened his lips from the water-bag, and relaxed. How long, he wondered, before Lobo made another move? An hour, two? He would not waste time now that the horses had been scattered and his party confined to progress on foot, but perhaps he already had reluctant travellers who would be in no hurry to sweat and strain over harsh mountain tracks.

Lobo's closest companion, the one he called Joe Jensen, would follow but with faint heart for the hunt. He had lost much of that in Lobo's finishing of the wounded man; witnessed the killing of his kind by one of his own. Jensen no longer believed.

The trappers would lose nothing of their greed for what they mistakenly saw as some reward from Lobo for their loyalty. But what had they to offer now that they had delivered the lawman? Little, save their guns, and perhaps a few more hours of heat and dirt, and growing fear might not rest so easy in their fingers, not to mention their stomachs. Bud Ziggers would have to do as he was told. No choice if he wanted to stay alive.

But how would the lawman react?

He had ridden into a rattler's lair of seething revenge in his pursuit of Lobo and would seek to be free of it at the first opportunity, just as soon as he was thinking straight again. An opportunity perhaps that was closer than he thought.

Ocachi flexed his shoulders, drew his fingers to tight fists, relaxed again and lifted his gaze to the clear blue skies, his thoughts drifting to how things would have been on such a day at the cabin . . . with his wife at his side, her smile, dance of her eyes, the promise in her closeness, a promise now no more, that lay in the mutilation of her body.

He wiped the line of sweat from his brow, eased himself away from the rocks and tightened the rope hidden in the scattering of dead brush and dirt. One more hour, he thought. He would wait just one more hour.

11

Lobo was plumb out of his mind, thought Randall, reaching for the next safe hand-hold on the rock slope, and it was beginning to show. You could see it in the fellow's eyes, in that fixed, gleaming stare where there never seemed to be a blink, and you could almost hear the jumble of crazed thoughts going on behind it, almost see the furnace of raging images.

See it too in the way he was climbing ahead of the others right now, as if everything depended on reaching the ridge of the slope, that he would find Ocachi there, just waiting to be shot, or worse. Well, maybe the 'breed scout would be waiting. Maybe not. Either way, Lobo would be the first to know.

Randall paused a moment to catch his breath, lick the sweat clear of his lips, turn his gaze away from the blaze of the sun, and was conscious in an instant of Jensen's fierce glare on his back. Hell, he was beginning to spook him a deal more than Lobo. Jensen knew with the instinct of a hunted animal when not to lose sight or sound of the hunter — and he was watching Randall every inch of whatever way they went. Maybe he was expecting Randall to make a break for it. He was right, that was just the thinking in his mind, but not yet, not here. No, Mr Jensen, you are going to have to wait!

'Move it, Marshal,' hissed the man, 'or I'll make yuh next breath yuh last.'

Randall grunted and climbed on.

* * *

Bud Ziggers felt the sharp prod of Salts' boot in his backside, winced, and for one crazy second thought of turning to spit in the mangy trapper's face.

One more time and he would, sure as this sonofabitch heat he would, and to hell with the consequences! Or was that

95

precisely what Salts wanted him to do? You could bet your sweet life on it! Well, maybe he would not get to giving the scumbag any such pleasure. Nossir, he would keep on going for just as long as this madman up ahead saw fit — or Ocachi called it a day, as he would, as he surely would.

Bud gulped, groaned and clambered on. And just what in God's name was Lobo figuring on now, he wondered? How long could he keep this up? Did he reckon on scouring the Moccasins for the rest of his born days? Did he really believe he could even out with Ocachi? Not this way, no way — on foot, out of food and water. Give it another two days and there would be nothing left of any of them, not a stitch worth the picking over.

The marshal, he reckoned, was figuring much the same. But he would make his break when he was good and ready, and Bud was planning on being right alongside him when he did, come what may. Fellow like Randall would find the edge soon enough. And you could bet your sweet life on that, too.

Meantime, Lobo had reached the top of the slope and was standing there like some godalmighty giant at the moment of conquest . . .

★ ★ ★

'Well, shift yuh butts, will yuh, f'Crissake!' roared Lobo, straddling the ridge, waving his Colt, glaring back at the others through wet, bloodshot eyes. 'We ain't here for no afternoon stroll, yuh know. Shift, damn yuh!'

'Just calm y'self, Rufus,' called Jensen, pausing in his climb. 'And get yuh head down before that 'breed fills it full of holes.'

Lobo growled and shielded his eyes as he gazed round him. 'He's out here somewhere,' he croaked. 'I can smell him. Maybe no more than a half-mile ahead. Up there in them rocks, I'd figure, skulkin' like a flea-bag jack-rabbit.' He spat ahead of him and wiped his mouth. 'Yuh reckon that, tradin'-post man? Yuh rate my thinkin'?'

Bud Ziggers raised his cracked, sweat-soaked face. 'I ain't got a clue,' he moaned.

'Well, yuh'd best get to findin' one fast,' snapped Lobo, 'otherwise yuh ain't no use and I'll rid m'self of the burden of havin' yuh around.'

'In hell's name — ' began Bud.

'Lay off!' shouted Jensen. 'Fella here's about as blind to where the 'breed is as the rest of us, so why don't yuh just rest up, Rufus, go calm y'self? We ain't doin' no good yellin' like brats save to tell Ocachi where we are.'

'As if he don't already know,' muttered Randall.

'Ain't askin' you,' drawled Jensen. 'Shut yuh mouth and keep it that way.'

'I'd reckon he's close,' said Salts to no one. 'Yeah, I'd say close.'

'How'd yuh know?' spluttered Blooney. 'Yuh don't know no such thing. Hell, Salts, yuh couldn't sniff a hog at ten paces, never mind a 'breed scout at a half-mile!'

'Who's sayin' I couldn't sniff a hog?' flared Salts.

'I am,' blinked Blooney. 'I'm sayin' so. Yuh never could and yuh never will.'

'Now you listen up there, Blooney — '

Jensen kicked angrily at the loose rocks. 'Shut up, all of yuh! Right now. Yuh hear?' He ranged his Winchester over the faces turned to him. 'First mouth that opens gets it lead-lined, so help me God!'

'That's the way, Joe,' bellowed Lobo from the ridge. 'Tell 'em. Spell it out, and don't take for no messin'. Had my way of it, we'd shoot the whole mangy bunch of 'em right now. Be done with it. Go settle that 'breed and ride clear of this hell-hole.'

'Yuh ain't goin' no place,' muttered Randall again through clenched teeth.

Jensen flashed the marshal a fiery glance and seethed quietly. Bud Ziggers wiped a lather of sweat from his face. Blooney grunted, Salts swallowed and stared anxiously at Lobo.

'Well, what we waitin' for?' called Lobo. 'Ain't doin' no good sittin' here burnin' up. Let's move.'

'We need water,' drawled Jensen. 'There'll be none of us fit for nothin' if we don't have water.'

'And water we ain't got,' said Lobo. 'F'get it 'til we take that 'breed, and then we'll go find water. Some creek-bed close, eh? That so tradin'-post man?'

Bud squinted into the shimmering glare. 'Let me tell yuh somethin',' he croaked through a long, dry swallow. 'Let me tell yuh straight, Lobo, yuh got about as much chance of findin' water out here as I have of walkin' backwards clear through to Kansas. There ain't no water. There ain't a creek or a crack that ain't brittle-bone dry, and the higher yuh go, lettin' Ocachi lead yuh just where he wants, the worse it gets, believe me. I been up there, mister, I seen it for m'self and it ain't no place for man or beast.' Bud swallowed again.

'Them's the facts of it, so if yuh wanna go ahead and shoot me — and the rest of us come to that — go right ahead. Do it now. Do it while we're still sittin' this side of Hell, but save the last bullet for y'self. Yuh'll be glad yuh did.'

Lobo's stare tightened like a beam of light on Bud's face. Blooney slapped his cracked lips. Randall folded his arms slowly. Jensen simply waited.

'Well, mebbe we are a mite ambitious,' said Salts softly. 'Mebbe we should go back some, find water, then get to the 'breed. Wouldn't lose more than a couple days at most. There's a creek far side of the pine range — '

Lobo fired a single shot that lifted stones and dirt at Salts' feet. 'No goin' back,' he glowered, 'not for nobody. And I ain't sayin' that again. Next time, the lead sticks. Yuh got it?'

Jensen sighed and cradled the Winchester. 'So where to now, Rufus? Yuh got it all figured?'

'Up there, the higher rocks scattered through that pine outcrop. That's where he's holed-up. I feel it in my gut.'

'And that ain't the only thing he'll be feelin' in his gut,' muttered Randall out of Lobo's earshot.

'Yuh beginnin' to annoy me, Lawman,' murmured Jensen. 'Yuh gettin' to be a real itch.'

'I'll be waitin' when yuh get to scratchin'!' grinned Randall.

Gentle Joe Jensen might then have crashed the rifle stock across Randall's face, might have barrel whipped him where he stood, but the moment passed in the sudden, eerie slip and slide of rocks and shale from the outcrop up ahead.

'Didn't I tell yuh?' bellowed Lobo, listening to the echo of the sound as if hearing inner voices. 'Didn't I say so? He's there. Right there.' He swung round to level his glare on Salts. 'You, get up there. See what's happenin'.'

'Me?' coughed Salts. 'Yuh want me to — '

'Shift, damn yuh!' roared Lobo. 'Shift — or die where yuh stand.'

12

Salts crouched, waited, blinked his one good eye, wiped the sticky sweat from beneath the patch at the other and swallowed on foul-tasting saliva.

Hell, what had he got himself into? How come he was dumb-headed enough to be lathered up, shaking and scared half out of his skin, alone on a hillside tracking a 'breed Indian scout for the satisfaction of a brain-buzzed madman who was going to kill him anyhow?

Hell, he had made a serious mistake back there in the pine forest. Should never have taken the lawman; should have stayed with the old boots meat and the cackle-berry blisters; should never have figured his luck had changed. When did a lifetime of bad luck ever get to slipping its skin for juicy steaks, silky sheets and soft women?

And, hell, he should never have reckoned on Rufus Lobo being anything other than what he was: a fat-bellied, gun-slinging sonofabitch with about as much decency in his tongue as a rattler had in its bite. Crazed with it at that.

Hell, too, he had dragged Blooney into all this — not that he was two cents to a tin can bothered about Blooney right now. He would have to look to his own hand when the deck spilled out. No, right now he was pondering real deep on just how he was going to slip clear of the 'breed up ahead *and* put dirt between himself and Lobo's venom faster than bug juice down a drunk's throat.

Way he was seeing it from here, a few yards short of the outcrop where the rocks had been disturbed, he had two choices. One, he could push right on into the outcrop and trust that the 'breed never saw him, let him pass, or had never been there anyhow and that the rock slip had been caused by some tracking animal. Two, he could try sneaking off to left or right and bank on Lobo not spotting him until he was out of gunshot range; then just keep on running.

No choice.

You could bet every stitch on your boots that Lobo had him fixed tight and was not going to take his eyes off him for one lousy moment. So he would have to go on, into the outcrop, through the scattering of pines, out the other side . . . and pray harder than a gospel sharp that he was still breathing when he made for cover. Maybe he could hole-up till nightfall, slip away in the dark, get himself back to the foothills, the plains; go find a horse, go any damn where!

Hell, it was no choice, but he had made it and now was the time to act.

He blinked and swallowed again, fingered the eyepatch nervously, ran his fingers through the brittle stragglings of his beard. No sounds, no movements up ahead or around him. Sun was high, sky clear, heat like a cauldron, air as fetid as a trapper's armpit, hardly fit to breathe, but he was, he reckoned, alone with only Lobo somewhere back there at the ridge watching him.

Darn right he was! He could feel his stare like a beam of the sun. Well, watch this, you old scumbag, watch me go — and with any luck that will be the last you will see of me!

But easy, he thought, beginning to move, no need to rush, not yet; time would come soon enough for the scooting. Trick was to treat this like stalking an animal — not that he had ever made a snorting success of that! — and take it all a step at a time. Lobo might be in a hurry to get this done and the 'breed out of his hair, but he was not the one sitting out here trying to figure the reason for that rock spill. Come to think of it, when was Lobo ever in the front line save when all the odds were with him?

No time to reckon on that; time only to move on, soft as a breeze, not a pebble shifted, not a stick of dead growth cracked.

He paused again, crouching low, the good eye flicking like a beacon, the sweat oozing out of him in sticky blots and trickles. But he was gaining ground, sure enough, easing ever closer to the scrawl of pines. Once into them, he figured, and he would be out of Lobo's sight. Then all he had to do was keep right on going, fast as he could.

But, hell, to where?

The good eye scanned the daunting range of mountains spreading like a mass of heaving limbs to the heavens. Into them, he wondered, swallowing again? Up there, to a coffin in the rocks? He grunted. Maybe not. Maybe he would head to the left, to what looked from here to be a maze of narrow crevices and gulches. That would be the place to disappear into till the sun went down and the air got cooler. Then, much later, on again, into the night . . .

He was closer now, almost able to reach out and touch the pines. And a mangy-looking bunch they were at that, half dead for want of water, scorched in parts to rust-red bones, some branches bent so low they might have been dipping their parched mouths to the earth as if to . . .

Salts was sure he had not veered a whisker from the faint track he was following; certain he had missed nothing out of place in the scrape of that impoverished land. But he had, and it was all too late when he came to knowing it and long beyond recall as he got to feeling it.

It was the suddenness of that dipped branch whipping into life that stung him first. One moment it was there, just another branch bent to the earth, in the next, as Salts' foot tangled with something taut and hidden from his sight, a swishing, slashing surge that crashed between his legs, crunching his groin, and hoisting him high into the air as if some wasted missile in a catapult.

He saw the sky like an open mouth,

the blaze of the sun, the very tips of the dehydrated pines; saw the world turn turtle, the light grow dark, the darkness sparkle, so that it seemed rocks were flying and dead brush racing, and then he was diving headlong from the whip of the branch back to the ground, to the jaws of the baked stone, and crashing to a useless, empty sprawl of limbs, crushed skull and blood that bubbled in the heat.

Salts might have said, come his welcome at the Pearly Gates, that he saw nothing in those last minutes save that crazy, swirling world. But he would have been lying through his broken teeth and tangled beard. Last thing Salts saw was a face, somewhere in the depths of a crevice, that was filled it seemed to him with eyes as bright as stars that simply mocked.

★　★　★

Rufus Lobo saw most of everything that happened; saw it with Joe Jensen,

Marshal Randall, Bud Ziggers and Blooney right alongside him, and when it was over and the silence and stillness settled again, turned on them like a wild thing catching breath.

'Good thing I sent him up ahead, weren't it?' he croaked, sniffing and then spitting lazily. 'Could've been any one of us out there.' He spat again. 'Still, we know where the sonofabitch 'breed is now, don't we?'

Randall stared at Lobo without the flicker of a movement across his face. Jensen twisted the toe of his boot in the sand. Bud Ziggers sweated until he thought he would melt.

'Salts,' murmured Blooney, his wet lips glistening. 'That was Salts. We been partnered up most of our lives. Never been nowhere savin' t'gether. Always t'gether.' His old eyes watered. 'We were like brothers.'

'Yuh got such a hankerin' for stayin' close, it can be arranged,' growled Lobo.

'For God's sake,' mouthed Randall.

110

Jensen dug his boot deeper into sand.

'We ain't goin' on,' said Bud, wiping his face.

'We can't, not into that sorta hell.'

'Always t'gether . . . ' mused Blooney, staring into space. 'Don't seem right he should go like that. T'aint right. T'aint right at all.'

'Ar, f'Crissake cut the moonin',' snapped Lobo. 'Fella's gone and that's the way of it. Should've looked where he was walkin'.'

'Damn you, Lobo,' groaned Blooney. 'Damn yuh eyes and the ground yuh stand on! Yuh ain't worth the spit that creeps outa yuh mouth! Yuh ain't worth nothin'.'

Blooney's lunge at Lobo stood about as much chance of troubling the man as a loose fly looking for a place to sleep. Lobo had stepped aside and brought a hatchet-chopping hand across the trapper's neck before he had moved a yard.

'Darn fool,' growled Lobo, kicking Blooney in the ribs. 'Good mind to settle him right now.'

'Leave it right there, Rufus,' drawled Jensen. 'Ain't nothin' to be gained by clutterin' the land with more bodies. Just leave it. We've all had enough. Time we tailed it outa here while we got the chance; before that 'breed gets to pickin' out who's goin' to be next.'

'Don't fool y'self he ain't already done that,' muttered Bud. 'I'd wager he's watchin' us right now. Somewhere up there . . . Behind any one of a hundred rocks. And yuh ain't never goin' to know which one, are yuh? Not 'til it's too late.'

It was almost too late for Lobo in the next ten seconds as a hail of rifle fire blazed from the rocks beyond the outcrop and he dived for the dirt like a suddenly spooked lizard.

Jensen hit the ground alongside him. Bud Ziggers fell back down the slope in a whirl of limbs and lathered sweat. Blooney groaned then slid away on his stomach. But when the firing was done and the silence heavy as a draped cloak and bewildered eyes danced in thudding heads, there was no sign of Randall.

The marshal, it seemed, had been spirited into nowhere.

13

Randall licked at the sweat on his lips, blinked through the haze of it across his eyes, and felt his fingers begin to relax in their grip on hot dirt. That, he reckoned, blinking again, had been about the biggest gamble of his life, and just about as crazy, but his luck had held for the few precious minutes he had needed, and now, damn it, he was out of Lobo's reach.

And maybe staring the next devil clear in the eye! He waited, listening, hardly daring to breathe much less move. Ocachi was all through with the shooting — for now — from wherever he was holed-up, but what had been the figuring behind it? A warning to spook Lobo into realizing he was close and watching, or a diversion? He had certainly not been shooting to kill — he could have done that with ease — so maybe he had intended for Randall and Ziggers to scramble free. Maybe he was flushing out Lobo and Jensen from the rest. Hell, did it matter?

Point was, where to now?

No chance of staying where he was, midway between the ridge where Lobo was keeping his head down, and the sprawling mass of rocks and crevices beyond the outcrop where Salts had fallen foul of Ocachi's trap. So it would have to be on to the rocks, trusting that the half-breed had him clear in his view and would keep Lobo pinned tight for as long as it took to reach safer ground.

Randall licked at the sweat again, risked a quick glance back to the ridge to be certain that Ziggers had not made it, and scrambled on, not stopping now until he had reached the outcrop and the cluster of gaunt pines.

He blinked and swallowed over his parched throat at the sight to his left of Salts' battered body, debated for a moment whether to risk retrieving the trapper's Colt, decided against it, and went on.

He had cleared the last of the trees and was settled into a bulge of rocks, taking time to mop at the sweat, ease the ache in his limbs, when he tensed at the sound again of sliding rock. Ocachi slipping away, moving higher? Hell, he was making a noisy job of it! Fellow with his instinct and understanding of the Moccasins must know a hundred tracks and routes through the creeks and gulches. Could hardly be a path he had not taken at some time, hardly a rock where his feet had not passed. No need for him to . . . Unless . . .

Randall tensed again at another slide, this time closer, thicker, lifting a mass of dust and dirt in its wake. He coughed, blinked, as the tumbling mass slid and skidded less than a body's length from where he huddled in the bulge, heard the crash of the rocks slipping by him and the gathering roar of a whole lot more behind them.

Goddamn it, Ocachi had let loose an

avalanche! Must have disturbed a crumbling ledge, disturbed an already weakened boulder. Whatever, this whole stretch of the rock face was suddenly alive and shifting, and if he was not smart enough and fast enough, all set to bury him alive!

★ ★ ★

Lobo sprang to his feet, dragging Jensen with him. 'Yuh see that, Joe?' he bellowed as the sweat ran like rivers over his face. 'Yuh hear that? That sonofabitch 'breed has sure as hell put a foot wrong — and some! Ain't he done just that? Ain't he just?'

A broad, sweat-soaked smile spread over Lobo's face as he watched the cascading rocks beyond the outcrop. Jensen wiped a tight, anxious hand over his face. Blooney slapped his lips and gaped.

'Oh, my godforsaken hat,' murmured Bud Ziggers. 'If Ocachi's caught in the middle of that . . .'

'And that two-bit, nosy marshal with him,' echoed Lobo, slapping his sides. 'Know somethin', Joe, I reckon we got ourselves an edge. At long last we got ourselves an edge.'

'Mebbe,' muttered Jensen, shielding his eyes against the glare as the tumbling rocks thickened and gathered momentum and the dust-clouds swirled. 'Mebbe we have at that.'

'No 'mebbe' about it,' beamed Lobo, 'I can see for m'self we got an edge. Clear as day. Yuh can bet yuh sweet life the 'breed's trapped in that and there ain't goin' to be a hope in hell of no 'fraidy hole for him out there. Not a hope.'

'Then mebbe we're all through here, eh?' croaked Blooney. 'Mebbe that's it and we can pull out, eh? What yuh say?'

'Pull out, f'Crissake?' boomed Lobo. 'Pull out? There ain't goin' to be no pullin' out 'til I got that 'breed's body right here at my feet. So I can see him, what's left of him, and torch the rest to the memory of Mitch and Clips. That's what we gonna do, soon as them rocks and dirt have settled some.'

Blooney closed his eyes. Bud swallowed and fancied his stomach had slipped to his backbone, and Joe Jensen simply stared at the rolling mist of dust that seemed to cloak the Moccasins like a shroud.

A death shroud.

★   ★   ★

Randall spluttered, coughed, thought for a moment he would choke, blinked on a darkening day of dirt, and winced at the crescendo of noise, the stinging pains across his shoulders, and wondered how long it would be before a rock finally found his head and crushed it.

Not long, he reckoned, not if it kept up at this pace. But a darn sight more to the point, how in hell was he going to summon the strength for one last effort to get free? Another shuddering slide of rock and he would be suffocated for sure. Maybe Ocachi had already suffered the same fate, or been crushed in the first slip. Maybe the pulp of him was trickling to oblivion right now. Maybe the blood would seep through the rocks to drip into Randall's eyes before they finally closed . . .

He spluttered again, felt his hands free — and, hell, he could still move his legs! If he could somehow hoist himself, get a grip on something that would hold fast for just long enough . . .

Maybe if he prayed . . .

The next slide broke to a thundering roar and grind, a grating creak and whipping, echoing snap that seemed to Randall to loosen half the mountainside in a storm of flying stone, rock, dirt and dust, and suddenly he was moving with it as if gathered up like some useless hulk of flotsam.

He was pitched to one side, rolled, thrown onto his back, then thrust forward in a ball of tight limbs, halted suddenly against solid rocks, shifted round it as if being swept away on some surging tide of dirt, bounced and thudded to his stomach to slither face-down to wherever the mass of the slide had come to rest.

There was a strange, unreal silence when Randall finally blinked and realized he was still breathing — God alone knew why, but he was! — and, with every last ounce of the strength left to him, just about able to move. The momentum of his slide had carried him clear of the main bulk of the rocks to bury him almost waist-high in the drift of dirt piled against the thicker, heftier slabs of rock. He was battered, bruised, cut and grazed across his arms and legs, and his head was thudding like a storm, his breathing wheezing out of him as if being forced through clogged earth, but there was nothing wrong with his vision, and there was no mistaking what he saw ahead of him.

He groaned inwardly at the sight of Ocachi sprawled unmoving in the dirt, and then aloud and from the pit of his stomach at the approaching bulk of a grinning Rufus Lobo.

14

'Lord works in mysterious ways, and I can tell yuh that for a fact. Yessir, mysterious ways ... ' Lobo sent a high line of spittle to a slab of rock and stared hard at the bodies sprawled at his feet. 'Take this situation for an instance. Now who would've thought — '

'Get to it, Rufus,' snapped Jensen irritably. 'Yuh got the 'breed, for what his half-alive body is worth, and we got the marshal. Now what?'

'Yeah, now what?' murmured Blooney. 'Can't we get to things? Get it over and get out, f'Crissake?'

Bud Ziggers held his gaze tight on Ocachi. Fellow was in a bad way, sure enough, but alive. A condition that was going to be about as short-lived as a blink if Lobo had his way. Same went for Randall, he guessed. Not a deal of hope for either of them, and the marshal sure as hell knew it judging by the look in his eyes.

Bud grunted quietly to himself. Something had to be done, and fast, before Lobo got to work and then settled the final score with Blooney and himself. Only two-bit hides going to ride out of this in one piece were Lobo and Jensen. And you could see *that* clear enough in Lobo's eyes!

Lobo aimed another line of spittle and settled the sprawl of his hands on his hips. 'Well, now,' he croaked, 'I got somethin' kinda special in mind for the 'breed. The marshal I ain't fussed over, just so long as he ends up dead and off my tail.'

'Yuh goin' to kill a lawman?' blinked Blooney. 'Yuh plannin' that? Don't rest easy killin' lawmen. They got long shadows. I seen times when fellas like that — '

'Cut the reminiscin', trapper,' glared Lobo. ''Breeds, lawmen, any kind on two legs, they all come the same, and stay as dead.'

Bud Ziggers shivered, Blooney swallowed, Jensen murmured something inaudible.

Lobo wiped the sweat from his face and stepped slowly round the body of Ocachi. 'This sonofabitch took out my partners, so I figure he should know all about what it's like to be dyin'. Feel it creepin' in, wishin' it'd hurry. And that's just how it's goin' to be — creepin' in with the ghosts of Mitch and Clips hauntin' him 'til the end, and then some. Just like that . . . '

* * *

Bud knew, in the next hour, that he was maybe going to have to risk what was left of his life if Ocachi was to have so much as half a chance of staying alive. And half a chance right now was being generous. But nothing else for it, he figured; who else was there to help? Blooney seemed to be doing things as if in a trance, part conscious of a hatred for Ocachi for the death of Salts, but a darn sight more spooked by Lobo. Staying within a spit of the sonofa- bitch's favours was how he saw himself surviving this hellhole — but, then, thought Bud, who could rate anything of Blooney's figuring in his state of mind? Right now he could look a rattler in the eye and see an angel!

Randall's options were nil. He was back to being trussed and dumped again, with a fast bullet being about all he could look forward to. But Jensen seemed in no hurry to settle the issue. Maybe he was saving the shooting of the marshal for a moment he could relish. Or maybe there was something more. Whatever, all Randall could do was squirm and wait — and not so much of the squirming if he wanted to stay cool in the afternoon heat.

Meantime, Lobo and Jensen were at work on Ocachi. They had humped and dragged the still half-conscious 'breed's body clear of the fallen rocks and dirt to a higher reach of the rock face and then on again to where a ledge skirted a sheer hundred-foot drop to the razored jaws of a dry-bed creek. Plan was, it seemed, to leave Ocachi somehow suspended over it in such a way that the more the fellow tried to loose himself the slimmer his chances of avoiding the drop.

Lobo had done the figuring. 'We ain't got a deal of rope, so we use what there is sparin',' he had grinned. 'We fix the 'breed with his arms round that boulder there, tie him tight as we can, then ease the boulder close as a hair to the edge of the ledge. Yuh see my thinkin', Joe? Soon as the sonofabitch comes to his senses, he's gonna move, and it's my reckonin' that a fella smart as him is goin' to realize it'll take just one false shift to send the boulder with him fixed to it hurtlin' down there to them mean-lookin' rocks. Now, he ain't goin' to be in no hurry to do that, so mebbe he'll just hang in there, sweatin' it out 'til either the heat or the cold gets to him, or mebbe he'll shrivel for want of water, or mebbe his weight'll get too much for the boulder — any one of half-a-dozen ugly options, eh, Joe?'

Lobo's eyes had gleamed. 'Don't matter a cuss which way, does it, fella's goin' to know he's goin' to die, real painful, slow as it comes? He's goin' to have time to think it all through, all alone and by himself. Time to remember Mitch and Clips, and me, Joe. He's goin' to see me, Rufus Lobo, right to the very end!'

Jensen had waited for Lobo's guffawing laughter to blow itself out before easing back from the edge of the ledge. 'And when we done all this,' he had said quietly, 'we just goin' to walk out, eh, all the way back to that tradin' post — without water and no prospect of it? Yuh figured all that along with everythin' else?'

'Sure, I have,' Lobo had croaked through a twitching smile. 'Sure, I have, and it's all goin' to pan out fine, just fine. We'll find water, that tradin' critter and the trapper'll lead us to it, yuh can bet. And yuh goin' to have that marshal to keep yuh occupied, aren't yuh? Yuh can have some real fun with him, eh, Joe, just like the old days?'

'There ain't no old days no more,' Jensen had murmured. 'We left 'em all behind at that 'breed's cabin, Rufus. Left 'em in that squaw's blood.'

'And that 'breed's payin' for it now, ain't he? Payin' for what he did to Mitch and Clips.'

Jensen had waited a moment, his gaze moving over the foreboding sprawl of the mountains. 'Well, somebody's payin',' he had murmured. 'But I ain't sure who or for what.'

Bud had heard all the planning and conversation between Lobo and Jensen and set to thinking just how in hell he was going to leave Ocachi with at least a hope — and drawn a blank before taking two breaths. No chance of doing anything against Lobo; no chance of looking to Blooney for help; Randall was out of action. What in tarnation was left?

The rope!

The thought slid into Bud's mind like something stepping out of the shadows. Supposing he could somehow tamper with the rope Lobo intended using to fix Ocachi to the boulder? There was only one short length of it between them — right alongside Blooney's pack — so could he get his hands on it, do something to it, maybe weaken it in some way? It was about as much of a chance as a snowflake stood in a heatwave, but it was all he had.

* * *

They walked away from that stretch of the Moccasins, back towards the outcrop where Salts' body would soon be crow meat, at the first hint of the evening shadows. They went slowly, silently, without a word between them, their steps barely heard over the rocks and through the cracked, dry brush. They might, thought Bud, have been the coming night's early ghosts, or the remnants of those with no place to go.

And no one looked back, not once, not until the outcrop had long since been swallowed in the darkness and the high peaks brooded like watchful heads on the backdrop of a moonlit sky. And by then it was too late.

There was nothing to see.

15

Ocachi saw the darkness like a hole into hell, and did not dare to breathe; so much as lick a lip or blink an eye. Even a sniff of the cold night air might be enough to shift the boulder the half-inch that would prove fatal.

The rock was cold now to his flesh, harsh and biting at the cheek pressed to it, his limbs stiffening against the strain of stillness, the bruising, cuts and grazing from the landslide beginning to burn, and the rope lashing him to the boulder already eating into him like the teeth of hungry spiders.

One slip, a hurried step over cracked rock, was all it had taken to loose the avalanche that had almost smothered the marshal and handed Lobo the edge he needed. Careless; a fool move that might yet be the prelude to his last — if this boulder shifted that half-inch.

Ocachi eased a slow, gentle breath over the rock and slewed the angle of his gaze to his left and the stretched contours of his arm. He dared not relax it a fraction, nor the fingers beyond his sight. If a muscle so much as trembled under the tension . . . But it would not. He would not permit it, as Red Eye had taught: 'Comanche teaching says there is more strength in the mind that seeks to live than the limb that wrestles to survive.'

Perhaps, thought Ocachi, recalling the lined and weathered face of the old chief, but it was not so easy to find such consolation from where he was roped. How long could he hold out? Through the night until daybreak? But what then? There would be no trapper, no passing drifter through these hills for perhaps weeks, even months, and by then he would be no more than bones.

Ocachi eased another breath and closed his eyes — and was almost instantly back with the haunting images at the burned-out cabin, then of Lobo, the mountains, the landslide, of dying. 'No!' he mouthed without a sound, opened his eyes and was once again with the boulder, the rope, the strain and pain and the night chill settling like thin ice.

Soon the cold mountain air would creep over him and he would begin to stiffen, then shiver. It would be the shivering that would rock the boulder . . . slowly to, slowly fro . . . at first like a whisper as dirt grains slid away, then with a creaking and cracking until he was straining with all his strength against the forward momentum that would fill his face with a final rush of bleak night air.

'No!' he mouthed again, and flexed the fingers of his right hand instinctively. There was a difference there in the tension of the rope, a slacker hold; something leaner and less biting in the grip. He stretched his fingers, curled them in on themselves like claws. The boulder moaned but did not move.

He relaxed, recalling those last

moments of Lobo, Jensen and the trapper strapping him to the boulder. He had been only semi-conscious, aware of the men around him through a blurred mistiness, but Ziggers had come closer as if trying to look into his eyes, to say something in no more than a hurried glance, a half stare. Ziggers had lingered only a moment before Lobo had bellowed some curse and shoved him aside.

But what had been the message in the glance? What had Ziggers been trying to say? A farewell? Or had there been something else? Something about the rope? Ocachi's fingers moved again. The boulder groaned. He felt the faintest shift of the bulk, as if it squirmed, but he also sensed the rope begin to give — at first with only the easing of a hair-thin strand, then another, another . . .

Ocachi waited, not daring to breathe, suddenly unaware of the chill. A line of sweat had broken on his brow. He blinked rapidly, his thoughts beginning to crowd and swim. Supposing the rope did snap and his right hand come free, would there be the time to unravel the rest of him from the boulder before it plunged to the creek-bed, or would he be dragged with it? How much strength did he need to break the weakened strands? Would one tug be enough, too much? Did he need to ease his hand free or make it one decisive move?

The gamble that might spark the moment of panic.

His eyes closed. The images drifted. He was a boy again with Red Eye, not yet tall enough to reach the chief's waist; watching him as they went to the hunt, trusting to the old man's experience, his understanding, the instinct that made him wait. But for what, when the prize had moved closer? 'It is the hunter who needs to be close, not the hunted,' Red Eye had murmured.

Ocachi's fingers flexed again, slowly, softly, like feathers shifted in a breeze. He sensed the parting of another strand. How many before the rope was weakened through? How long?

The tightness at his wrist was easing, the fingers moving without effort, but the boulder's groans were deeper, protesting, threatening.

He blinked the sweat from his eyes, held his breath, gritted his teeth. Now! Two seconds and he would have his answer — the right one just in time, the wrong one all too soon.

*　*　*

Ocachi's right hand came free of the grip of the rope in one, decisive tug, but with the freedom came the sudden shift of his weight to the left and the groaning roll of the boulder. No time now for subtlety or thinking things through; no time either to wait. The boulder began to slew on its base as Ocachi leaned back, heaving against the natural momentum of the bulk to plunge to the creek. His free hand grappled wildly with the coils around his legs and back to his still fixed left hand, pulled and yanked in the blind confusion of not knowing whether he was tightening the rope or loosening it.

Sweat clouded his eyes, pain flared and burned through his limbs; the night seemed to fill suddenly with the flashing dance of the moonlight as he swung his body to left and right, heaved and leaned back against the grinding weight of the boulder yawing ever closer to the abyss.

The sounds of his grunts and groans and the scraping, cracking crunch of rock cleaved the darkness like a knife-blade slashed through taut canvas, but now Ocachi knew he was gaining as a leg came free, then his left hand, until only the sheer weight of the boulder was pinning the rope to his right leg.

This was the moment when he knew he must let the bulk roll on and trust that it did not drag the coil with it. He relaxed, flattened the palms of his hands on the rock, felt the boulder begin to slip and slide beneath them

— then spread his arms and fell back.

There were seconds when it seemed the bulk had come to a halt, when it would not roll clear of the rope and Ocachi would have to risk pushing it, seconds when he waited breathless, his stare wide-eyed on the boulder's face, when he might have yelled at it to move.

And at last it did, gathering life as if in one great shudder before groaning like some tortured beast to the lip of the ledge and plunging soundlessly out of sight.

Ocachi was on his feet when he heard the final splintering crash, the echoing roar as the boulder shattered in the creek-bed's jaws, and he did not move until the sound had passed and the night closed in again. Only then did his eyes gleam in his thoughts of where the new day might begin.

16

'Yuh hear that? That was the boulder crashin' clear. Goddamnit, should never have left the fella like that. We should've done more.' Bud Ziggers' whispering faded on a sigh as he leaned back against the cold rock face and scanned the high night sky. 'Did my best, though. Guess it just weren't enough.'

Randall stared for a moment into the face of Joe Jensen where he lounged in the shadows on the far side of the narrow creek, wondered if he too had heard the low rumble from the distant peaks, then glanced quickly at Bud. 'Yuh get to the rope?' he murmured. 'Yuh fix it?'

'Tried to,' hissed Bud, 'savin' that Lobo had his eyes glued to me most of the time. But I might've done enough — if Ocachi got to figurin' it.' He sighed again. 'Darn me if I don't just take my chances right now and go drop a rock on that sonofabitch's head!'

'And yuh wouldn't get further than Jensen's gun,' grunted Randall. 'Lobo might be sleepin', but Jensen's all eyes.'

Bud squirmed against the rock face. 'To think of Ocachi goin' like that . . .' he mused. 'Hell, t'ain't human. Lobo ain't a man, he's some sorta screwed-up monster. Maniac, gotta be.'

'Yeah, well, definin' what he is ain't helpin' right now,' said Randall. 'We gotta get to plannin' what to do before we finish up his next helpin' of pulped meat.'

'Tell the truth, mister, I ain't thinkin' straight no more. Just can't get my mind workin' round where we are, what we goin' to do, when we goin' to do it . . . What about that fella Blooney there? What's Lobo goin' to do with him, f'Crissake?'

'Kill him,' croaked Randall. 'Just as soon as he's used him up and he's no more than baggage. Mebbe next time we hit water — 'ceptin' that Blooney won't get closer than spittin' distance of it.'

'*If* we hit water.' Bud's gaze settled on Randall's face. 'Know somethin', mister, we got about as much chance of stumblin' into a waterin'-hole as we have of findin' ourselves guns and horses, and walkin' out of this hell country is just as fanciful. Even if we get lucky some how, some place, Lobo'll be hoggin' it all for himself and Jensen. Let's face it, we don't figure none in Lobo's reckonin', savin' as crow meat.'

'Which is why — ' began Randall again, and fell silent as Jensen approached from the shadows.

'Don't reckon on that 'breed bein' an itch no more,' he drawled from behind a slow grin. 'And I ain't sorry about that.' He paused a moment. 'Leaves us with y'selves and that trapper, don't it? 'Specially you, Marshal. Yuh been buggin' me a whole lot since we cleared Passmore, and I ain't taken with the prospect of seein' yuh around much longer, so puttin' yuh to rest up here seems like a reasonable notion, the tradin'-post fella alongside yuh. But I guess yuh already figured that for y'selves, eh?'

'Sorta,' clipped Randall.

'Tell yuh one thing — ' croaked Bud.

'I'm sure yuh can, old-timer,' grinned Jensen, 'but I ain't for listenin'.' He eased his weight to one leg. 'Yuh got 'til sun-up. Might as well let yuh see what sorta day yuh goin' to be missin'.' He backed away slowly. 'Sun-up,' he nodded.

'Now I'm gettin' to thinkin' straight,' gulped Bud when Jensen had retreated to the shadows. 'Seein' things real clear. Same go for you, Marshal? Seems to me we got only one choice — we make a break for it soon as we can. We're either dead in two yards or dead in two hours. Now ain't that a cheerin' thought!'

But Randall was not smiling.

★ ★ ★

142

Blooney slapped his lips, ran his tongue over his gums, and fixed his tired, bloodshot eyes on the snoring, sleep-twitching bulk of Rufus Lobo. Fellow sure made a racket even when he was flat out! How come a scumbag like that could sleep so deep, anyhow? Would have figured for him waking at the crashing roar of that boulder back there in the mountains, relishing the last of the 'breed. But, hell, the fellow had just kept right on snoring!

Well, maybe the dead would be back to haunt him in his nightmares, not that Lobo had too many of them, you could wager. Too darned cold-blooded for that. Still, there had been a look in that 'breed's eyes that would have spooked most men; a sort of lingering stare that burned right through, like a slow, hot poker boring through a fellow's skin. And Lobo had seen it sure enough, no mistaking that; seen it and held it for just as long as it took for the sweat to break on his brow.

Blooney shivered and swallowed on

his gritty throat. Hell, it had sure been a bad day's work when Salts had persuaded him to tie in with Lobo. Should never have gone along with it; should have figured Lobo for what he had always been, what he would always be — a louse-crawling sonofabitch. And there was a deal worse to come. Hardly needed a crystal ball to see where things were heading from here: that marshal, the fellow from the trading post, and himself were headed for the big dirt, dead as bleached bones come sun-up.

But not without a fight. Nossir! There was no way old Blooney was going down without making his mark. Lobo and Jensen might well be figuring they would be the only two to walk out of these godforsaken mountains, but the shadows at their backs would be long and chilling. You bet!

Trouble was, Jensen had taken his gun and his blade — had that knife a lifetime — and there was not a hope in hell of getting to a horse for days, so any escape would have to be fast and on foot, with the equally troublesome prospect of no water to head for. Still, freedom had a high price. You paid up and took your chance.

But when, he wondered? First light, an hour before — or why not right now while it was still dark, while Lobo was sleeping and Jensen just lounging? Might be as good a time as any; get clear into the hills before Jensen had a target to shoot at; hole-up 'til daybreak, then . . . He would get to figuring that when it was fitting.

Blooney stretched, yawned, nodded sleepily at Jensen, waited till the man had relaxed again, then tensed himself. It was going to have to be now. This very minute. Or never.

* * *

Randall nudged Bud Ziggers out of his doze. 'Blooney,' he hissed, 'watch him. I figure for him makin' a break.'

Bud blinked, twice, then eased

himself away from the rock face. Darn it, the marshal was right, Blooney had all the look of a man set on scooting, and real fast. But, hell, how was he going to clear Jensen's guns, and just where was he going to run to; just out there, into the night, into nowhere?

'Here's our chance,' hissed Randall again. 'Soon as Blooney breaks, we go with it. Jensen can't shoot everywhere at once, and Lobo ain't stirrin'. Yuh ready?'

'Where we goin', f'Crissake?' whispered Bud.

'Anywhere. Don't matter none, does it? Just try to stay close, and keep goin' — 'til yuh drop.'

Bud blinked again, swallowed, felt the trickle of sweat at his neck, damp and sticky in the palms of his hands. Damn it, this was no way for a fellow of his age . . .

Then Blooney was moving.

Sprung into life like a jack-rabbit. Running low, twisting, turning, slithering over the ground as if blown across it by a whirling wind — but going the wrong way, damn it, heading over the longest distance to the deepest dark.

'Shift!' croaked Randall, and shoved Bud clear of the rock at the first blaze of lead from Jensen's gun and the sight of Lobo struggling out of sleep.

The shooting was fast and accurate once Jensen had taken in the situation. He paid no attention to Lobo's manic rantings and concentrated his first volley of fire on Blooney, pinning the trapper to the dirt with a blaze that opened a gaping wound in his thigh and following through with a second from which the fellow never stirred again.

Randall groaned as he flung himself to the deepest shadows, and again as Bud Ziggers tripped, lost his balance, sprawled helpless against a boulder and was suddenly smothered by the lunging bulk of Lobo who settled Bud's bid under a hail of thudding punches.

Randall plunged on, blind now to the ground ahead, bent double against the snarling, snapping shots from Jensen's gun, arms outstretched against the pitch darkness as if feeling for some place to part it.

He was conscious of racing to a slope, going down, down to only God knew where, then of sand and shale at his feet, a tangled mass of dead brush threatening to pull him back, of smoother rock, a sudden ascent, and then of some narrow gully that closed in like the cold stone walls of a prison cell.

The silence took him by surprise. No more firing, no crash and crack of chasing steps, no voices, nothing save the hiss of his own breathing, the thud of his heart. Randall waited a moment in the grip of the gully, wiped the sweat from his face, listened, peered into the darkness, his thoughts spitting round his mind like sparks. Blooney, he guessed, was dead, but what about Bud?

'Hell!' he croaked, looked back, groaned and pushed on into the suffocating night.

There was nowhere else to go.

17

Bud Ziggers' face felt like it had exploded: eyes so bulged and puffed he could hardly see out of them; a nose flattened and broken across his cheeks; a mouth that rattled with loose teeth — and all that, he thought, swallowing slowly, without mention of a chin too bruised to touch and a head throbbing like a week of dust-bowl tornadoes.

Hell, he was in a mess, and maybe too weak now to move, if moving was what that sonofabitch Lobo had in mind. Only consolation was that it seemed Randall had got clear — God knows to where or to what purpose, but free, and that was some hope. As for Blooney, looked like Lobo was going to leave him for the crows where he lay face down in the dirt.

Bud swallowed again, winced, and focused through his eye slits on the misty drift of the morning light. All was still, all quiet, save for the low murmurings coming from Lobo and Jensen over there at the edge of the creek. Hard to tell at this distance what they were saying or plotting, but he could sure as hell make a good guess.

' . . . he ain't goin' to get far. No chance. No water, no gun. No hope, if yuh ask me. Yuh figure?' Lobo's gaze was hard and fixed on Jensen's face.

'Mebbe,' drawled Jensen, 'but I wouldn't — '

'Damnit, Joe, that fella still spookin' yuh? Yuh should've settled with him long back, same as we did with the 'breed.'

Jensen's eyes lifted slowly to Lobo's face. 'Did we? Yuh sure about that?'

'What yuh sayin', f'Crissake?'

'Reckon it,' said Jenson. 'We left the 'breed back there lashed down on that boulder, and sure we heard the sound of that same boulder crashin' to the creek-bed, but did the 'breed go with it? We weren't there to see it, Rufus, so we

can't be certain, can we? Ain't nothin'
to say — '

Lobo spat deep into the dirt.
'Goddamnit, if I don't get to whippin'
some sense into you, Joe Jensen! What
the hell yuh tellin' me now? How come
yuh mind gets to flippin' round yuh
head like a whiskey-addled whore? How
come, eh? Ain't we done just what we
said — got to that 'breed and settled
him? Sure, we lost Clips, but mebbe no
loss way his thinkin' was twitchin' him;
and sure we had them mangy trappers
tryin' to suck up to us, but we settled
them too, ain't we? And that marshal
— heck, like I say, he's a no-hoper out
there on his own, ain't he?'

Lobo wiped the dribbles of saliva
from his lips. 'Now figure it, Joe: we
walk outa these hills right now, this
mornin', and we drag that busted
tradin'-post critter with us. Least he
knows the way, and when we're out, we
finish him too, just like the rest. Then,
Joe, then we get to restin' up a coupla
days before we go find ourselves some

easy livin', eh? Some good food, good drink, real nice girls ... Place over at North Forks — '

'Randall will be followin',' mouthed Jensen softly. 'Yuh bet yuh life he will. Feel it in my bones.'

'So?' sighed Lobo, easing his weight to one side. 'He ain't armed, is he? He comes within a spit of us and we down him like we were stalkin' dumb turkey. Simple as that.' Lobo grinned. 'Trouble with your bones, Joe, they need some loosenin' up. Yuh know, shakin' down, get that dust and mountain chill out of 'em. Nothin' one of them sweetmeat girls over North Forks way — '

They heard the crash and roar of tumbling rock reach over the silence of that early morning as if some hidden beast had broken free of its lair and rushed a mountain in its anger. Heard it and stood rigid and open-mouthed as the echoes spilled around them like a chorus of hollow screams.

It was close on a full minute before Lobo spoke again. 'And just what in hell's name was that?' he croaked.

'T'ain't what it was yuh should be askin', Rufus,' murmured Jensen. 'It's *who* it was.'

* * *

Randall squirmed from the rock cleft like a dazed lizard. He winced against the bite of morning chill, blinked on the strengthening light, blinked again, focused, and lay full length on the cold ledge watching the pall of dust and dirt far below him.

'Sonofabitch,' he whispered to himself. 'Sonofagoddamn-bitch.'

His eyes narrowed and squinted as he watched the cloud curl and drift to merge with the spread of breaking sky like a breath. Unless his climb to this place through the night had scattered his sense of direction and whereabouts, that rock fall down there was at the head of the creek where he had left Lobo and Jensen. Chance, coincidence, the hand of Fate? Unlikely, he reckoned. Bud Ziggers? No strength in Bud for starting a crash like that, even supposing he had slipped clear of Lobo. So that left . . . Ocachi? Could it be that the half-breed was on the move again? But if that were so . . .

Randall squirmed a foot higher, peering hard now into the creek as the cloud began to thin. No sign of anyone. Nothing moving. No sounds either. Fellow passing through might have figured the fall for just a mountain waking restive.

But not Randall.

He squirmed again so that now his head and shoulders were above the cover. Worth the risk, he reckoned; worth Lobo spotting him — he was out of gunshot range, anyhow — just to get a glimpse of . . . hold it, Lobo and Jensen were on the move, scrambling like black ants towards the fall. Would only take minutes for them to realize their easy way clear of the creek had been closed. Only chance for them now was either to climb the fall or go find some other route. Not so easy. Not when you are out of water.

Randall licked his cracked lips. Water — no hope of that right now. Forget it. Concentrate. Watch the fall. Watch Lobo, damn it!

The light was full as an open eye and the first of the sun glare streaming across the hills and mountains before Lobo and Jensen seemed to grasp their situation. 'Took yuh long enough!' murmured Randall, holding his gaze steady. 'Now what?'

Lobo was pointing to the higher reaches, Jensen's gaze following the sweep of his arm. They planned on climbing out of the creek, skirting the worst of the fall, then pushing on through the rock and brush to the distant sprawl of pines. One hell of a climb, thought Randall, especially in the heat of the day and their thirst beginning to tighten in their throats. But what about Bud, and maybe more to the point, what about Ocachi? Still no sight of him, still nothing to indicate that he might . . .

No, wait, he was wrong, there was something — more like somebody. The drifting shape of a man high on the ridge of the range to the west. No more than a silhouette from where Randall was positioned, but no mistaking the identity. That was Ocachi out there, sure enough, and he was making no effort now to stay hidden.

Damn it, the fellow wanted to be seen! He was baiting Lobo again. Coming back from the dead like a spectre to haunt and taunt.

Randall blinked, swallowed, and slid back to the cleft. No question now of where he needed to be. No question either of what he needed to do.

* * *

'So help me, next time I get my hands on that 'breed I'll skin him — and he won't be dead while I'm doin' it!' The sweat on Lobo's burned, weathered face and through his blackened stubble glistened like a dusting of silver. His eyes were wild, bloodshot, wet with staring, and now his whole body shook and rumbled with a rage that threatened to consume.

Jensen watched him from the creeping shade of a boulder. Plumb out of his head, he mused, scuffing his boot slowly over the dirt; eaten with obsession and squirming in the jaws of it. Fool could hardly see straight, let alone think clear. Next hour, he figured, was going to be a mite difficult.

'We'd best pull out,' said Jensen carefully. 'Could make the far range back of us before noon.'

Lobo swung away from scanning the peaks for the drifting shape of Ocachi. 'Back of us,' he croaked. 'What yuh mean *back of us?*'

'Just that,' said Jensen, raising a watchful eye. 'Slip away to the east and track out to the plains from there. Chances are we might just fool the 'breed long enough to get clear.'

'What's all this *slippin' away, gettin'*

clear talk?' snorted Lobo. 'Yuh dumb or somethin'? Thirst gettin' to yuh?'

'Only thinkin' straight,' shrugged Jensen. 'Ain't taken with the thought of facin' out that 'breed, 'specially while that marshal is still crawlin' about.'

Lobo kicked viciously at a rock. 'Yuh been the same all through, ain't yuh? Right from the start. Backin' off like yuh'd got a fungus liver. Always backin' off. No stomach for settlin' with the 'breed and spooked rotten with that scumbag Randall. That's been it, ain't it? Just that. No reckonin' for Mitch and Clips. Nossir! And mebbe none for me when it comes to it. Ain't that the top and bottom of it, Joe?'

Jensen eased himself slowly to his full height and levelled his gaze. 'Talkin' through yuh hat again, Rufus. All mouth, no sense. Yuh just don't get to thinkin' things through, d'yuh? Not since Mitch died. Blinkered, that's yuh trouble, fella, plain blinkered. So let's get to some facts, shall we?'

'Yuh just listen — ' fumed Lobo.

'No, Rufus, this one time you listen, 'cus I ain't spillin' it out again.' Jensen slipped his thumbs to his belt and relaxed.

'The 'breed ain't dead, nothin' like it and it don't matter a jot how he came to stay alive. Fact is, he's up there and dealin' all the cards again. New deck, Rufus, with four aces for the 'breed. Got it? Now, my reckonin' says he means to kill us, somehow, some place. He ain't armed, but I don't figure that a problem in his case. Problem is ours. Got it? So we high-tail it outa here fast as we can, 'cus if we don't, we're dead.' Jensen sighed. 'Yuh lost, Rufus. For once in yuh life, yuh lost, but you're still breathin', so yuh hold tight to that. Got it? So we f'get the marshal for now, f'get the tradin'-post fella, and just shift our butts outa this neat little trap the 'breed's sprung for us.'

Jensen turned his back on Lobo and swung his gaze over the peaks to the east. 'There's a cut in the rocks 'bout a mile to the right,' he murmured. 'We could make that before — '

Joe Jensen's view of the peaks, the cut, the lifting light and glare of the morning were darkened in the instant of the thud of the Colt butt across the back of his head. Seconds later he lay at Lobo's feet like a body sprawled there, too weary to take another step.

'Lost, eh?' croaked Lobo. 'So yuh figure I lost? I don't never lose, fella, not never. *Got it?*' But the satisfied sneer on Lobo's face had faded when he scanned the range again for a sight of Ocachi.

There was no one there, save what might have been the shimmer of a passing ghost.

18

Ocachi knelt, waited, listened, ran a hand over the smooth coolness of the rock, then eased forward with all the stealth and silence of a hungry snake.

He slid quickly into the next cradling cleft between boulders and raised himself to tighten his gaze on the creek below. The rock fall he had created had worked well, stopped Lobo and his partner from whatever plan they had in mind and forced them to think again — not that Lobo had seemed to do a deal of that. Not his way, like so many of his kind, and now he was intent again on climbing back into the mountains, this time alone.

Ocachi frowned. Jensen would have to be left where he lay unconscious. Perhaps Randall or Ziggers would get to him before he was thinking straight again. It was of little concern with Lobo stumbling wild-eyed and sweat-soaked towards him. So be it. Let him come. Let him struggle on until he was worn, sun-scorched and exhausted.

Red Eye had used the ploy often enough in those early days of being hunted by the rough-riding land grabbers. 'He who chases must do the running. You will learn, Ocachi, to stay ahead with the time to rest and see your way. It is the one who follows who must be worn until his feet are as stone and his sight clouded like the mist. Only then, when you have led to the ground of your choice, will you turn and wait. Only then . . . '

Ocachi grunted and leaned back in the cleft, his eyes closing in the calm of rest. The effort of freeing himself of the boulder and creating the fall had taken its toll. His muscles ached with tiredness, his head throbbed, and the images of loss flared across his thoughts like flame. Where now was the comfort of his woman's touch, the fingertips that stilled dull pain; where the

162

closeness into gentle dreams?

He stirred suddenly at the sound of a slip of rocks far below him. Lobo. He grunted again and listened. Give the man a few breaths longer, then move on. He ran a finger under the darkened shadow belly of the boulder to gather the still lingering film of dawn moisture from the surface and licked at it slowly. It was good, but a pity weapons did not come as easily! No matter, he would have to trust to his instincts against Lobo's bullets.

Then he slid away like a shadow.

*   *   *

Goddamn the sonofabitch, how come the 'breed had got clear of that boulder, cursed Lobo through his thoughts as he scrambled over the rocks? Somebody tamper with that rope? Had to be. That trading-post critter, for sure. Well, his time would come soon as this was done. Yessir! Meantime . . . The 'breed had no gun, no more of them sickening

163

arrows. It would be like shooting at pinned-down flies once he got a sight of him. All over in an hour, maybe less. Then he would show Gentle Joe — show him the scalp of Ocachi! How about that?

He reached for another rock hold, slipped and cursed again through a clenched-teeth hiss. Steady there, Lobo, he told himself, keep it easy, easy, no cause for rush; that 'breed is all slowed up some place, darn near exhausted, you could bet. Maybe he was no more than yards away, figuring on just how he was going to dodge hot lead when it started blazing. No dodging them, fellow, no way. Best you might manage is dance to them while it amused, then the last one, straight between the eyes.

To hell with Joe Jensen, he thought, scrambling again. Who cared, anyhow? Joe was getting old, too slow, all washed up, seeing scumbag lawmen round every rock. Time he went to his veranda, got himself a rocker and stayed put with his thinking. That had always been Joe's loose spur — his darned thinking. It was doing that got a fellow moving. No place for a warm butt in Rufus Lobo's reckoning.

He slipped again, paused, and watched the rocks tumble away behind him. Hell, it was hot up here and he could sure use water. But not yet, not by a long shot. A whole heap of go still waiting to be called on. Time for water when the time was right, when that 'breed —

Damn it, there he was, slipping clear of them boulders like a randy rattler. Too far away for a shot. Best not to waste good lead. Later, later.

'Just keep goin', fella,' croaked Lobo. 'I'm right with yuh!'

★　★　★

Randall pulled Bud Ziggers deeper into the shade and settled his head and shoulders against the cool rock face. 'Yuh ain't goin' no place, fella,' he said tightly. 'Nowhere. Yuh understand?'

'Tell the truth, marshal don't reckon I could right now. Not like this,' groaned Bud through a long, tired sigh. 'Leastways, not 'til — '

'Yuh stayin' put. Right where yuh are. Lucky I happened across yuh.' Randall wiped the sweat from his neck. 'Sorry I can't keep yuh company, but I gotta get to Lobo and Jensen before they close in on Ocachi.'

'Tell yuh somethin', mister,' groaned Bud again, 'yuh stackin' tall odds against y'self, aren't yuh? Hell, yuh ain't even armed! How'd yuh figure — '

'I ain't figurin' nothin', not that close. Last sight I had of them rats they were reckonin' on which way to go. Lobo'll want Ocachi, and Jensen'll be somewhere in his shadow. Me, I'll just be there wherever it is. With luck.'

'And yuh goin' to need a whole helpin' of that! Hell, I ain't never seen nothin' like this, and that's for sure. Still, we got this far, but if I ever get outa this — '

'Don't put too much store by it, not yet.'

'So what's yuh plan?' winced Bud, stretching back against the rock. 'Better be good.'

Randall swung his gaze to the peaks. 'Ain't got one, save to get out there — get to Lobo.'

'Yuh must've one helluva score to settle, mister. Yuh sure it's worth it? We had any real sense, we'd be staggerin' outa here best we could. We'd mebbe get to water far side of this creek. Three days walkin' and we could be on the flat.' Bud relaxed, his arms loose at his sides. 'And I shouldn't go givin' Ocachi too much concern. If there's one man can take care of himself up here, it's Ocachi. It's his country, Marshal. Ain't none know it better. Yuh seen that for y'self. And now he's on the move again . . . Hell, am I glad that rope snapped for him when it did.'

Randall's gaze had tightened. 'Yeah,' he murmured, 'so am I. It's kept Lobo here, and I got a notion I know just where he is . . . ' He glanced quickly at Bud. 'Stay put. I'll see yuh later.'

'How much later?' called Bud to Randall's disappearing back. 'Or mebbe never,' he added when the marshal had gone.

★   ★   ★

Gentle Joe Jensen heaved himself into the cover of rough brush and boulders and ran a hand slowly over the back of his head. Hell, it was sore, about as sore as his thoughts raging behind the pain.

Just a glimpse of Lobo, one measly glimpse, and the lead would fly, fast, accurate and for certain. There was only ever one way out for a mad dog, and that sonofabitch had set his course for it plumb and clear.

Jensen grimaced as his hand came away from the wound. Time had come to call it a day, anyhow, he thought, settling his hat, more so with the loss of Siers and Monaghan. End of the partnership, end of the trail, but maybe

168

not quite yet, not until Lobo was finished and put to rest, for his own good, and before he grovelled like a crazed has-been in a hail of law lead. Or before that 'breed got to him. Only decent thing to do — the *last* decent thing to do. And the sooner the better.

Jensen tapped the butt of his Colt and waited a moment, listening for a sound, some hint of where Lobo might be climbing. Darn fool was sure to be rattling round the rocks like a bullet in a tin can. Might never occur to him to —

Jensen tensed, eased lower. There was a sound out there beyond the brush, a soft, slow, slithering sound that was far from the scramblings of a spook-brained madman. No, this was something very different. This was the creep of a man on the hunt who knew where he was coming from and going to.

This was Marshal Jim Randall!

19

Lobo gulped on the thick, sticky air and groaned over the grating soreness as he swallowed. Thirst was tightening up some, getting to him; thoughts of water when a fellow was clean out of it could get to jangling his nerves, set his mind spinning. Next thing he would be seeing things. But right now he wanted to see only one thing — that sonofabitch 'breed.

Damn him! How come he could disappear so easy; melt away like that sun-up mist; and how come he could do it without making a sound, not so much as a pebble disturbed? Fellow came and went like a ghost. But ghost he most definitely was not. Not yet! Time for that was a way ahead; another hour, two, who cared? It could take all day, two days, a whole goddamn week — saving that the thirst would be real sore by then.

Or could it be the fellow had not moved at all? Supposing he was no higher than that ridge up there, tight in the boulders, nursing the aches of his escape and setting up the rock fall. Possible. Could be he was fooling with all that loping around like a young mountain lion, just out of firing range. Maybe he was as drained as anybody out here. He was human. He got tired. He had a thirst like any other man. Well, if he was fooling, if he was figuring . . .

Lobo twitched at the sudden movement ahead of him. There he was, darn it, sidling out of cover like some shadow, waiting a moment, staring, looking him straight in the eye, would you credit, like he was tempting Lobo into moving, almost asking him to move. Fellow had some guts, say that for him, a damn sight too much for his own good. Nobody played around with Rufus Lobo like that!

Lobo had half raised himself from the

rough brush, drawn his Colt, tightened his stance, narrowed his eyes, when he saw Ocachi lift a boulder high above his shoulders and hurl it down the drift towards him.

The boulder hit the ground with a splintering thud, bounced and hung on the air like a grotesque severed head, crashed to the ground again, bounced, then raced on in a swirling curtain of dust and dirt and rocks.

Lobo was rooted where he stood for only seconds, just long enough to feel the onrushing grit begin to tingle and bite at his nostrils, scrape at his lips, before he ducked and fell flat in the brush, a torrent of dirt and stone pouring over him. He heard the boulder's final crash, the rush and groan as it broke apart to scatter itself in a shower of missiles; felt a larger, thicker rock thud into his spine, flatten itself on his backside, a tide of dust bury itself in his neck.

The morning was silent, thick and hot again when his face twitched and trembled out of the dirt, and he blinked. The dust was settling below a grey drifting light and glaring sun, but the ridge lay sharp and black and empty against the clear sky.

'Sonofabitch!' croaked Lobo, and spat. But nothing save dry dirt left his mouth.

★   ★   ★

It had been the crash and rush of the boulder that broke Joe Jensen's concentration, made him move, raise a sound and stiffen Randall's creep towards him.

There was a half minute when neither moved again, hardly dared to breathe, when they were poised only yards apart like two snappy bucks disputing a territory. Jensen ran his tongue over his cracked lips and let his fingers idle over the butt of his Colt. Randall was conscious of the sweat trickling down his back, his thoughts thudding round the puzzle of how it was that Jensen — and, hell, it could only be Jensen buried in cover out there — had separated himself from Lobo. Or the other way about: Lobo high-tailed it out of Jensen's reach. Whatever, Jensen was armed, and the odds stopped there.

He risked a quick glance to the mountainside. All quiet; no movements; no sounds of Lobo; nothing of Ocachi. But was Lobo aware of Jensen at his back, of Randall, and was Ocachi watching all three of them from up there like some slow circling hawk?

He blinked and concentrated on Jensen again. Nothing for it now. Somebody had to move before this sun shrivelled them all to dead roots. Time to take a chance, make a fast lunge for Jensen and trust his hand was not too frisky on the butt of his Colt. Maybe he would get lucky.

Randall sprang from cover like a leaping leopard, but without the leopard's keener sense of what he was springing to. Randall had no idea. He simply rose, sweat-lathered, wild with anger, the frustration of being trapped in the mountains, and flung himself to where he had reckoned Jensen was waiting.

Not so.

Randall clawed empty air, saw only a blur of the bright light, then fell with a sickening thud full length into the hollow among rocks where Jensen had crouched. He gasped, blinked furiously, spat dirt and was swinging round on his butt when the hot, probing metal of a gun barrel on his chin stiffened him tight as an ice block.

'Oh, my, Marshal,' drawled Jensen through a wide grin, 'I'd have figured yuh for knowin' better than to move like that. Careless, Mister Randall, real careless.'

Randall sat perfectly still, the barrel pressing hard against his flesh. 'I didn't get lucky, that's all,' he murmured. 'T'ain't over yet, Jensen. Keep that in mind.'

'But I think it is, Marshal. Fact, it's gone on 'tween you and me for too damn long, from way back there at the Passmore. Should've finished it first time round.'

Randall raised his eyes to Jensen's face. 'Well, then yuh'd best get to it while yuh got the chance. It'll be yuh last.'

* * *

Ocachi narrowed his gaze on the drift of the rocks far below. The lawman was in trouble, bad trouble, and had maybe only minutes before Jensen tightened his finger on that trigger. His gaze moved quickly to where Lobo still lay solid as a log to the ground. No trouble there for the time being. It would take Lobo a while to gather himself and summon the courage to climb on. That left the lawman counting every breath.

Ocachi's gaze narrowed again. Only one chance, he decided, as his fingers slid to the buckle of his belt. Just one, as Red Eye had shown on that day they had scattered the herd of stolen cattle grazing their lands. 'No need to tell the world that we are here,' he had said, 'simply to tell the beasts that danger is.'

Ocachi slipped the belt clear of his waist, looped one end of it back through the buckle and reached for a rock, weighing it carefully before lodging and tightening it in the sling of the belt. He took a last look at the men below him, then came slowly upright, whirling the belt above his head until it swished and scythed the air to whistling shreds.

He waited, sensing the momentum, the gathering weight of the rock, then, with a final whirl with his arms stretched at full length, the muscles bulging, released it and watched it fly across the light, climb as if winging to the sun, and begin its streaming descent to the ground like a comet thrown from the heavens.

It seemed long minutes to Ocachi before the slinged rock approached its target. Did it come silently, he wondered; was Jensen aware of it, or was his concentration on the lawman too intense; did either hear it, or did it crash a yard to the left of them with all the shock and surprise of a giant ghost's footfall?

He waited only long enough to see the lawman seize his opportunity as Jensen's concentration broke and he grabbed at his gun hand. There were seconds then when the men tumbled away in a heap of writhing limbs, when he could almost hear the grunts and groans of their desperation, when they were locked and coiled like snakes in a fight to the death, then he kicked another rock towards Lobo, raised his arms to the sky and shouted his defiance as if calling on all the devils in creation to do their worst.

The echo lingered like a haunting.

20

Lobo clawed at the dirt until his fingernails were split and broken and blood was bubbling at the quicks.

'Sonofabitch devil!' he mouthed, grinding his teeth over dust. 'That's what he is, damn him — a devil! Well, he ain't draggin' this one into no fiery furnace, and that's for sure. Nossir! I'll see him into Hell first, so help me I will.'

He raised his smeared, grimy face a fraction above the tumble of rocks and scanned the ridge. Not a sight of him now. Nothing. Just the ridge, the sky and that damned sun. He grunted, then eased round to gaze over the reaches below him. No sign of Jensen and that lawman either. Pummelled the life out of each other for certain. Darned fools. Wasting good energy when there was that 'breed to settle with. Well, leave the pair of them to the crows, that was his thinking. Who gave a damn anyhow? Not him!

He went back to watching the ridge. That 'breed might be smart — all that figuring his belt for a sling, all that heaving rocks — but fact was he was as naked as a babe when it came to the real thing: no gun, no blade, no arrows. No hope! Not a snowball in hell's chance once he came within range of a gun. Lobo's gun!

He grunted again and eased forward, dragging the dull, damp, sweat-soaked bulk of his body over the dirt like some fevered slug. Might take a while, might take a whole half-hour, maybe an hour, to reach that ridge, but when he did — oh, boy, when he did! — watch your back, 'breed, you might turn round to see another devil, one with a Colt in its hand!

'Yeah,' he croaked, 'can see the look on yuh face now. See it like it was right there, just top of that goddamn ridge . . .'

*   ⋆   ⋆

Randall took the blow full in the face, saw the blood spray like a sheet of rain, the darkening shape of Jensen loom like a cloud, and fell back across the rocks. The breath left him in a whistling hiss, a grumbling groan, and then he was shaking his head, blinking, wondering how long it would be before Jensen scrambled to wherever his Colt had been tossed. Maybe he had no idea; maybe the surprise of Ocachi's hurled rock from the ridge and Randall's lightning attack had blinded him to where he was, what he was doing. But not completely, he thought, rolling to his left as Jensen closed again, fists as tight as stone, eyes blazing.

Randall kicked out, felt a boot make contact, heard Jensen's groan, and was rolling again towards the open space of scrub. Get to your feet, get to your feet, damn you, he yelled inwardly, as he winced at the snagging cut and grab of bone-dry brush. He shook the sweat from his face and peered through blurred, swimming eyes at the flattened bulk of Jensen just below him. Fellow still had not found the Colt, was twisting to left and right in search of it, running his hands through dirt and massed scrub, but with one eye on the marshal as he saw Randall come to his knees, then slowly, unsteadily to his feet.

Randall flung himself forward, arms outstretched, hands reaching for whatever he could grip of Jensen. His fingers fastened on the man's shoulders and for a moment he was staring directly into Jensen's eyes, seeing the fury there, the burning anger, feeling the hiss of hot, fetid breath, watching the lips curl to a snarl. The grip was short-lived as Jensen stiffened and thrust Randall aside as he might brush a fly from his shirt.

Randall was down again, hands in the dirt, blood dribbling from his mouth, legs beginning to buckle. Hell, just how much more could he take; how much more had he got to give? Not a deal, not if Jensen's next lunge . . . But the man had tripped, snagged a boot between rocks and was losing his balance.

Randall squirmed, twisted, spat blood and was tensed to launch into another attack when a glint in the scrub to his right flashed across his eyes. The Colt! Jensen's gun, there, not a body's length from him, just waiting for a hand to reach, fingers to grip. He plunged towards it, saw Jensen's eyes flick in the same direction, spot the glint, recognize it — and then the scrambling, skidding race was on!

Randall had the edge, no more than a fingertip as Jensen's hands clawed at him, tightened on his shirt, ripped the cloth clean away, fell clear and clawed again. One last reach, thought Randall, just an inch. His fingers straightened, lengthened until he thought the bones would snap. Closer, closer . . . The sweat was pouring from him, staining the dirt, mixing with the dribbling blood. Jensen was groaning, cursing, summoning every ounce of his strength for another grip, one last effort to fasten his fingers like a manacle on Randall's arm.

The marshal reached again. Less than an inch now, just a pebble's width from the butt of the gun. Another reach, this time with a shuddering heave of his body, a convulsing thrust of muscles, but Jensen's fingers had settled on flesh, were tensed to close in a vice-tight grip.

And then he had it! Fingers on the butt, flattening, pinching, clawing until the moment of fastening.

Randall heaved again, dragged his legs clear of Jensen, and twisted round like a seething snake, the Colt firm and steady in his hand. 'Not another breath, Jensen,' he croaked in a voice that grated like ground rock. 'Don't even think it.'

Jensen gasped, gulped and lay still, his stare unblinking on Randall's face. 'I wouldn't wait if I were you, Marshal.

It's always a mistake.'

Randall's finger tightened on the trigger. The shot would burn clean through the man's forehead, end his life in an instant when he would hear the sound of death roaring in and see the light divide as if the sun had exploded. 'That homestead, them folk,' he murmured. 'The 'breed's woman, and all the rest far back as yuh can remember. This is for them.'

'Yeah,' drawled Jensen, licking at sweat, 'I figured so. Said as how yuh were a long shadow, Randall. I was right.'

Randall's stare narrowed. The sweat on his face glistened. The blood at his mouth began to dry and harden. 'Long as the longest night, Jensen,' he hissed. 'And it's only just beginnin'.'

And then his finger eased away from the trigger and he smiled cynically.

★ ★ ★

Lobo spat and glared at the rim of the ridge until his eyes were burning with the sprawl of it. Hell, it was like the edge of the world and never seeming to get closer. But that was no cause for not pushing on. Nossir! Place just had the look of being far; another few minutes, shade more scrambling, sweating, cursing, and he would be there.

'Breed must have found an easier route, he reckoned. Made no difference. When Rufus Lobo set his mind to something, it stayed that way. No going back, no giving in. 'Breed would do well to dwell on that, take good note. Time was fast coming when he would get to feeling it. And that was all it was, just a question of time.

It was full noon when Lobo topped the ridge and stood there swaying like some outcrop growth caught in a slow breeze, his gaze wandering aimlessly over the lift and fall, pitch and reach of the rock faces ahead, his throat trembling in the pinch of its dryness. No sign of the 'breed, not a breath, not a whisper of him. But he was there, sure enough. Oh, yes, right there. Maybe just watching, wondering how long he had left to him.

'Not long, fella, not long,' muttered Lobo, shuffling on to the next incline, then halting, swaying again, squinting into the searing light at the echoing sound of the piercing cry from the peaks ahead.

He could make no sense of that; seemed like the 'breed was calling to him, urging him on. Sonofabitch had about as much sense of hunting as a dumb hound starving in a snowstorm!

21

Randall was not sure even now that he had done the right thing. Fact was, and would always be, that Gentle Joe Jensen deserved to die. Now or later was about as academic as you could get. Territories 200 miles in any direction would all opt the same way: get rid of the scum anyhow you like, any place, only do it, for the good of all.

But Randall had backed off at the crunch moment of the best chance he would ever have. And he might just get to regretting that weakness; either learn to live with it, or die looking it clear in the eye.

He wiped the sweat from his face, blinked over his blurred, swimming vision, and prodded Jensen forward. 'Just keep movin',' he croaked, watching the man stumble over the sprawl of the rocks.

'Yuh goin' to rue this day, Marshal,' murmured Jenson. 'That yuh surely are. And yuh know somethin', I reckon yuh doin' that already. Now ain't that so, Mister Randall?'

'I ain't listenin', Jensen, so yuh can save yuh breath.'

'Ah, but that's just what yuh are doin'. That's the whole crux of it. Maybe not listenin' to me, save with only half an ear, but listenin' all the same — to y'self. True? Ain't I right?' Jensen half turned and let a slow grin crack his dirt-caked face. 'Reckon so. See, the way I figure it yuh should've shot me back there when yuh had yuh chance. 'Stead of that, yuh chose this way: keepin' me alive and pushin' on into these godforsaken mountains in the hope of roundin' up Lobo and takin' in the pair of us for a hangin'. Now ain't that just lawman thinkin'? Ain't it just? 'Bout as fool-headed as — '

'Cut it!' snapped Randall. 'This is my show from here on, Jensen. Yuh play it my way. Got it?'

'Sure,' grinned Jensen, stumbling on. 'Sure I got it. I ain't arguin' with that Colt there in yuh hand — yuh might get to usin' it next time round — but I'm sure as hell thinkin' and watchin', Marshal. Oh, yes, I'm doin' that, and deducin' real fast.' He halted a moment to swing the sweat from his brow. 'T'aint goin' to work, Randall, not this way it ain't.' He turned slowly. 'Yuh know that, don't yuh?'

Randall's lips tightened along with his grip on the Colt. 'Figure what yuh like, I ain't interested,' he croaked.

'Suit y'self,' shrugged Jensen. 'Like yuh say, your show, but if it were me there in your boots, I'd leave Lobo to Ocachi, get the hell outa here. Place ain't done nobody no good since we hit them foothills, and it ain't for changin'.' Jensen's eyes narrowed. 'And how much longer do yuh reckon we can hang on without water? Yuh thought of that, Marshal? Lobo ain't worth dyin' of thirst for, is he?'

Randall's lips tightened again. 'You'll hang, Jensen, Lobo right alongside yuh. The rest don't count for a damn.'

'Yuh reckon?' sighed Jensen. 'Well, I sure as hell took yuh for bein' smarter, that I did. Yuh come a long way, Marshal, and it might be all for nothin'.' He wiped a hand across his face and scanned the shadowed roll of the peaks. 'So we push on, eh?' he grinned. 'Like walkin' to a funeral parlour, ain't it?'

★ ★ ★

Lobo slithered down a slope of hot, stinging shale, cursed and came to a thudding halt at the base of a brooding rock. 'Sonofabitch!' he spat, and winced on the pinch in his throat. 'Sonofa-*goddamn*-bitch! The whole mangy country!'

He leaned back on the rock and closed his eyes against the unrelenting glare. Maybe he could rest up a minute, he thought, swallowing carefully, just long enough to gather himself, ease the aching limbs, get to thinking straight, listen out and watch for that devil 'breed. Damn it, he shifted like some spooked shadow, always there but always out of gunshot range? Never got to taking an aim on the bastard. How come? How come he could always be just out of range?

What the hell, he would make a mistake soon enough. Fellows always did, always went that step too far, pushed their luck. Never push your luck unless you wanted it to fall flat on its face! Lobo smiled softly to himself. 'Yeah,' he groaned, 'that's it . . . ' There was that time back on the Pake spread when that gunslinging youth name of . . . what was his goddamn name? Forget right now, but anyhow there he was, all lathered up one morning . . . or was it afternoon? Don't matter, there he was, whoever he was . . . 'Yeah, what was the sonofabitch's stupid name?' he groaned again, and was shaken out of his meandering at the sudden scattering of the shale as a length of brush root stabbed like a spear only inches from his thigh.

Lobo swung clear of the rock, came to his feet, drew his Colt and scanned wildly over the rocks for a sight of Ocachi.

'Got him!' he croaked. Right there, far side of the bluff, loping away like a leopard. Hell, out of range again! But maybe he could catch up if he ran, kept running. That was all it needed — just keep on going.

Lobo was still running for the bluff when Ocachi left it and climbed higher.

★　★　★

Ocachi dropped to his knees behind the jut of rocks, relaxed and settled his gaze on the man. He ran like someone out of his head on cheap whiskey; like a man not seeing straight, veering to left, to right, almost in a circle. Good, he thought. Then the time would come soon. One hour at most.

His gaze moved away to the more distant reaches of a long, winding gulch and the sight of the lawman and his prisoner making their slow tracks towards him. Not so good. The lawman should have turned back, trailed his man east, collected Ziggers and headed for the plains. But now he would have it in his mind to hunt down Lobo, complete his catch.

He would be disappointed.

Ocachi's gaze returned to the running man. He would let him come on until he had reached the bluff then turn him to the steeper rock faces. 'Weary your prey until it has no heart, then take it on ground where it has no hold,' Red Eye had whispered on those hunting days. 'Waiting is the only weapon you will need. You will be at your bravest with it when it's all you have. Learn it well.'

Ocachi grunted. He would wait.

★ ★ ★

'Know somethin', Randall,' said Jensen, halting again, 'I'd figure for Ocachi bein' somewhere up there. Sittin' easy in them rocks top of the bluff. Yuh readin' me? And yuh know somethin' else, I'd figure for Lobo bein' right on his tail. Yuh reckon?'

Randall cleared the sweat, let his arms hang loose, and squinted into the glare. Maybe Jensen was right, maybe this was as far as Lobo would make it, but getting to him ahead of Ocachi would not be easy.

'So how yuh plannin' on gettin' there first?' asked Jensen as if echoing the marshal's thoughts. 'Can't go no faster, leastways I can't, and I sure as hell ain't waitin' on yuh while yuh go fetch the fella. Kinda awkward, ain't it? Told yuh it'd get this way.'

Randall fumed quietly at the smug grin on Jensen's face. It got an inch wider he would wipe it clean away, permanently! 'Just keep movin', fella, that's all the figurin' yuh need to do.'

Jensen shrugged and turned back to

the rough track. 'Tell yuh somethin' else, Marshal, he called casually, 'I'm about all through with this. Had enough. Sweated through with it. So the real figurin' — '

Jensen swung round sharply and launched himself at Randall like a hawk in a swooping attack. And the Colt roared while he was still in full flight.

22

Randall's instinctive response sent the shot high and wide of Jensen's shoulders, a wild, scattered blaze that did nothing save to unbalance the marshal against the rushing bulk of his prisoner. Within seconds the two were tangled once again, a threshing twist of limbs; heaving, groaning, grunting and sweat-lathered, with Jensen always gaining the edge in his sheer desperation.

But Randall might even then have turned the odds had Jensen not reached for a rock, closed his fingers on it, raised it and crashed it across Randall's right hand still clutching the Colt. The marshal groaned in the agony of the pain and rolled away, leaving Jensen the few vital seconds he needed to scoop up the gun, come to his feet, leer cynically at Randall and stumble away, scrambling to the mouth of the gulch like some fever-crazed animal.

Randall saw him go through his blurred, sweat-swimming vision and wondered why in hell the fellow had not finished him then and right there.

★ ★ ★

Lobo had skidded and slithered to a halt and sunk exhausted to his knees at the crack of the shot. What the hell now, he mouthed, without a sound escaping his thirst-strangled throat; that two-bit marshal again; that all washed-up Gentle Joe doing his darnedest to scoot free? Somebody should put the pair of them out of their misery. Maybe somebody would if either of them got in the way of his reckoning with Ocachi. And no messing!

Lobo had waited there, still on his knees, his eyes squinting, blinking, peering over the towering rock wall ahead of him for a full two minutes. No hint of the 'breed, not a sound of him. Sonofabitch had gone to ground again, slunk away to wait his chance. Well, he had best not get to settling himself too easy; time was running out and this was going to be all through long before the sun slipped behind those peaks. You could bet on it!

And another thing . . . But Lobo had never got to it as he turned sharply at the sound of crunching steps, somebody running towards him. He came to his feet, shaded his aching eyes against the glare, swayed and tried to swallow. Hell, it was Jensen, pounding out of that gulch like a hound with a thorn in its butt. Must have settled with that marshal at last. So now what? What did he want, and why was he waving that Colt like some excited kid? Was he fixing on using it?

Too right he was! He was all spook-headed mad. Sun and that marshal had got to him, worn him down, not thinking clear save that he was heading straight this way, and with only one thing in mind.

Lobo stiffened. Well, he guessed he

might have known it, seen it coming. Joe had always been close, a darn sight too close, always hankering for taking over, running the show. He had that way with him, and gotten a whole lot worse with the years. So now he figured on being the last of the bunch, did he, figured on finally heading things up, maybe getting some younger guns around him, being the big man? Not so, Joe, not while Rufus Lobo still had breath!

Joe was moving slower now, walking, gun hung loose at his side, eyes fixed straight ahead. Typical. That was Joe's way. Seen it a hundred times. He got mean in a killing mood. Hell, supposing the 'breed was watching all this . . .

Lobo flashed a quick glance at the rocks. Nothing moving. No sounds. 'Breed was resting up. Well, no time for that here. His eyes squinted again. Joe was mouthing something, trying to shout, curse more like. Never could fathom that slow drawl of his. But no mistaking the look in his eyes; sad, empty, like he was pitying him. Pity, for Crissake, that was all he needed right now! All he needed was time and being alone to bring that 'breed to heel. Joe had never seemed to understand that, just never fathomed it. Well, maybe he would fathom this . . .

* * *

'Call it a day, Rufus, let's pull out, get ourselves clear of these mountains, back to where we belong. We can make it. I figured a way.' Jensen's words were shaping in his mind only to escape as whispers from his mouth. But they sounded right. Surely Lobo could hear them, knew what he meant? 'Yuh all through, Rufus. Yuh need to rest up. I'll fix it, same as I always did. Remember? Sure yuh do. I'm yuh partner. Long-standing. Best part of our lives. So let's leave it, friend, and get out. Let that 'breed be. He ain't worth — '

Gentle Joe Jensen never did under-stand why Lobo drew his gun that way, like he was meaning to use it, why he steadied it, levelled it, aimed so carefully, let it blaze. Never did figure why the shot hit him clean in the heart and turned that glaring sun-soaked day to such a long, cold, empty night.

Must have been a mistake, just a slip of the finger. Easily done. But, hell, Rufus, he had thought, you might have taken a mite more care. Always were a headstrong type. That had been the trouble all along . . .

* * *

Randall had been too late by a whisker. Joe Jensen lay dead and Lobo was scrambling on towards the peaks by the time he had ripped the sleeve from his shirt, bound his crushed hand and finally staggered clear of the gulch.

Lobo was out of his mind, had to be, to kill Jensen like that, and slipping deeper into his madness if he reckoned for an instant he could reach Ocachi. But maybe he could be stopped even now; maybe there would still be a neck for hanging if he could somehow get to him, get his hands — hell, only one hand! — on him. He had carried the law this far, one more effort was neither here nor there, not if that homestead and the folk murdered in it still meant a thing. They did. The hell they did!

Lobo was staggering on, slipping, sliding, sometimes moving in circles as if completely lost, then coming back by some inner sense to a straight line, veering away now from the sprawl of the bluff towards the sheer faces of the mountain range.

Fellow could hardly be figuring on scaling them, thought Randall, gasping, wincing, sweating as he followed. No chance; would never manage so much as a first hand-hold. Not a hope. But with Lobo clear out of his mind, seeing nothing as impossible or beyond him, who could say? Somebody had to stop the fool! But at this pace, at this distance, Randall was always losing ground. Had to make more of an effort, he reckoned. Find the strength. Get closer. Damn the man!

But just where was Ocachi?

★ ★ ★

'Yuh get y'self down here, 'breed,' hissed Lobo, staggering to a halt in the loose rocks at the foot of the sheer faces. 'Just quit the dodgin'. Get to bein' a man, yuh sonofabitch! I ain't leavin' 'til yuh do. Might as well get to it, fella, I ain't goin' away. Kill yuh just like I did that yellowneck back there . . . '

Lobo coughed and tried to spit. Nothing there. Only dust. Damn it, what had Gentle Joe been reckoning on coming up like that? Might have known he would be a loser. Well, some fellows always were, born losers from start to finish; never stood a chance. Bit like that 'breed up there.

'Hey, fella,' called Lobo, his cracked, broken voice echoing round the rocks like a strangled groan, 'yuh callin' it a day? Yuh all through? Finished? Had enough? Say this for yuh, though, yuh sure give a fella a chase for a two-bit 'breed. Say that I will. Yessir! Only me left now, yuh know. Imagine that — whole damn bunch cleaned out savin' for m'self. Yeah, just me, old Rufus Lobo. He don't go down so easy, does he? Yuh figured that? Bet yuh have. But I can't save yuh, fella, can't let yuh get away with doin' for Mitch like that. Yuh gotta pay — so let's get to it.'

Lobo coughed again, reeled, staggered, waved the Colt wildly, blinked on his blurred, bloodshot eyes, felt his lips stiffen and tighten across his teeth, the sweat burn through his shirt. 'Yuh comin'?' he croaked again. 'Yuh makin' a move? Ocachi, yuh hearin' me, f'Crissake?'

He swung round at the sudden crunch of rocks behind him. That damned lawman, still treading in his shadow, still gnawing away like a bad toothache. Well, his time was all through too. Right now! Lobo blazed the Colt, saw nothing of where the shots were aimed, felt only the shuddering jolt of the gun, then the shadowy shape of the lawman, one minute there, the next gone.

'To hell! To hell with all of yuh, every last sonofabitch!'

Lobo had turned again to the rock faces when the skies on that morning seemed to darken on the topmost ridge; darken as if some monstrous hawk had settled there, black as death, waiting its moment to swoop.

Lobo stared, the Colt hanging lifeless at his side, his parched mouth open, eyes wide, the strength trickling from his limbs like the sweat down his back. He saw the black shape move, watched it tense, its arms spreading; saw the mane of hair dance on the light, then stood without moving as Ocachi dropped from the ridge, his voice lifting like a haunting screech until its echo smothered the peaks.

There were long moments of being

flattened breathless to the rocks, of feeling Ocachi's weight crush him, his breath burn into his face, and then of the hands taking his throat between them, the fingers tightening, the life being strangled from him. The last clear sight he had before the light exploded were of the man's eyes filled, it seemed, with the flickering lick of flames, burning bright red and orange, and behind them the face of a woman, her lips parted in a slow, silent, satisfied smile.

Rufus Lobo heard nothing of Ocachi's cry to the heavens when the flames were no more.

23

'We all through here? We goin' home? Don't say we ain't, 'cus I might get to killin' yuh right here and now!' Bud Ziggers took a tighter grip of the rope rein to the mount and stared hard at Marshal Randall riding alongside him. He looked about as bad as Bud felt.

'Yep,' said Randall, 'we're goin' home. Ain't no more to be done here, save to find Ocachi.'

'And yuh ain't gotta deal of hope of that, not yet yuh ain't. He ain't goin' to show himself 'til he's good and ready. Always been the same — just takes off when he figures it's right. Up there in the mountains some place. Yuh'd never find him.'

'No, I guess not,' sighed Randall. 'Wanted to say our thanks for these horses he snaffled away from Lobo's hitch-line. Kept them well hidden.

Them and the water. Just about saved our lives, I reckon.'

'Didn't figure I was seein' straight when I came to and found them right there at my side,' murmured Bud. 'Ocachi must've slipped 'em close while Lobo and Jensen were stumblin' around in the hills. And thank the Lord he did! No mistakin'.'

Randall sighed again and grunted. 'Yuh reckon Ocachi'll just walk out when he's ready?'

'I reckon,' said Bud. 'Just like that. And yuh won't never know.'

'Might never see him again.'

'Oh, yuh'll see him again, sure enough. Yuh can bet. But when and where . . . who knows? Yuh don't predict where a fellow like Ocachi's concerned. He'll go his own way, in his time, with his thoughts, and they ain't none too healthy, savin' that Lobo and them scum are dead and gone. Amen!' Bud slapped his lips. 'Back to my flea-bitten mattress, I reckon. What about you, Marshal?

Headin' back east?'

'South,' said Randall. 'Callin' it a day. Gettin' too old for marshallin'. Had my share, and more.'

'Yuh can say that again. Yep, yuh can say that again . . .'

They had ridden on some miles when Randall reined to a halt, turned and gazed back over the shadow-hugged sweep of the Moccasins. 'Know somethin',' he murmured softly, 'I just get the strangest feelin' that somebody up there's watchin' us. Yuh get that feelin'?'

'Sure I do,' grinned Bud. 'Had it all along, from way back. Ain't you?'

But Marshal Jim Randall never answered. There seemed no need.

THE END

We do hope that you have enjoyed reading this large print book.

Did you know that all of our titles are available for purchase?

We publish a wide range of high quality large print books including:
Romances, Mysteries, Classics
General Fiction
Non Fiction and Westerns

Special interest titles available in large print are:
The Little Oxford Dictionary
Music Book, Song Book
Hymn Book, Service Book

Also available from us courtesy of Oxford University Press:
Young Readers' Dictionary
(large print edition)
Young Readers' Thesaurus
(large print edition)

For further information or a free brochure, please contact us at:
Ulverscroft Large Print Books Ltd.,
The Green, Bradgate Road, Anstey,
Leicester, LE7 7FU, England.
Tel: (00 44) **0116 236 4325**
Fax: (00 44) **0116 234 0205**

Matt Matthews had carved his ranch out of the wild Wyoming frontier. But he had his troubles. The big blow of '86 was catastrophic, with dead beeves littering the plains, and the oncoming winter presaged worse. On top of this, a gang of desperadoes had moved into the Snake River valley, killing, raping and rustling. All Matt can do is to take on the killers single-handed. But will he escape the hail of lead?

THE WIND WAGON

Troy Howard

Sheriff Al Corning was as tough as they came and with his four seasoned deputies he kept the peace in Laramie — at least until the squatters came. To fend off starvation, the settlers took some cattle off the cowmen, including Jonas Lefler. A hard, unforgiving man, Lefler retaliated with lynchings. Things got worse when one of the squatters revealed he was a former Texas lawman — and no mean shooter. Could Sheriff Corning prevent further bloodshed?

CABEL

Paul K. McAfee

Josh Cabel returned home from the Civil War to find his family all murdered by rioting members of Quantrill's band. The hunt for the killers led Josh to Colorado City where, after months of searching, he finally settled down to work on a ranch nearby. He saved the life of an Indian, who led him to a cache of weapons waiting for Sitting Bull's attack on the Whites. His involvement threw Cabel into grave danger. When the final confrontation came, who had the fastest — and deadlier — draw?

McKINNEY'S LAW

Mike Stotter

McKinney didn't count on coming across a dead body in the middle of Texas. He was about to become involved in an ever-deepening mystery. The renegade Comanche warrior, Black Eagle, was on the loose, creating havoc; he didn't appear in McKinney's plans at all, not until the Comanche forced himself into his life. The US Army gave McKinney some relief to his problems, but it also added to them, and with two old friends McKinney set about bringing justice through his own law.

BLACK RIVER

Adam Wright

John Dyer has come to the insignificant little town of Black River to destroy the last living reminder of his dark past. He has come to kill. Jack Hart is determined to stop him. Only he knows the terrible truth that has driven Dyer here, and he knows that only he can beat Dyer in a gunfight. Ex-lawman Brad Harris is after Dyer too — to avenge his family. The stage is set for madness, death and vengeance.